# Where the Woodbine Twineth
## & the Sycamore Ceased to Bloom

By William "Buck" Godfrey

Stellium Books

Grant Park, Illinois

William "Buck" Godfrey

Cover Design by Annette Munnich

# Dedication

The talented and beautiful Fulani: Bailey "Beans", Gabrielle "Gabby", Carter "Scrappy", Morgan "Captain".  My grand-daughters.

William "Buck" Godfrey

# Introduction

Death: transition to the heavenly realm; the end of life as we know it; a punishment for evil deeds; a Gentleman caller; a well-earned rest from life's turmoil; the Grim Reaper; the rider of the Pale Horse in Revelation; the Death Angel; the guest of the grave; Adam's and Eve's penalty for disobedience. The discussion of this phenomenon is varied and sometimes difficult.  However, it is a fairly accepted fact that when one is born, he will eventually die, except, of course, for the biblical Enoch and Elijah. Nevertheless, the inexplicable idea of Death is truly fascinating and provides a thematic thread that binds the works of this book.

Ironically, the book's title Where the Woodbine Twineth and the Sycamore Ceased to Bloom has an interesting take. The reader may ask where did it originate? Research indicates that it is found in the poem Prisoner of Perot by Estelle Lewis in the mid 1850's and appeared as an episode entitled "Where the Woodbine Twineth" in the Alfred Hitchcock hour where a black doll Numa comes to life.

Be that as it may, the author's use of the title stemmed directly from his father, William

Sr., who would always jokingly respond to someone's death in this manner: "Bubba, he's gone where the woodbine twineth and the sycamore ceased to bloom." Of course, that made sense to me. For sure, the dead person was seen no more talking, jiving or drinking in the neighborhood.

Even more enthralling is the intended title of the book should be The Strange Case of Moses Holms, the featured story in the work. As chance would have it, the "featured story" did not reach a length commensurate to be termed a book. However, the quality of Moses Holms is such that the publisher suggested that other material with a similar theme be added in order to ensure the work's recognition as a valid expression of scholarship and acknowledgment in the area of death, the paranormal, the Gothic, the phantasmagoric. This task was not as daunting as it seemed in that the author only had to create one short story. The other material he had at the ready.

First came The Widow Dart, a study in vampirism where the unlikely victim is male rather than female. The setting is a remote New England village where a simple ad in a newsletter leads to "marriage" and doom. The Watcher of Cut Bridge Road, the new entry, is a truly delicious narrative which explores hoodoo forces that exist in certain sectors of this country. Many people dismiss the machinations as outlandish, that is, until an inexplicable act occurs, usually tragic, which cannot be logically explained. And so we discover the redoubtable protagonist, Hester, who had one eye that is hazel and the other which is either gray or black, who sees "things" and events not privy to others. She and her "familiars" are constantly observing the hypocrisy of life, the futility of love and introduces the reader to Wiccan symbols and language as they serve to mete out "justice" on an unwitting husband.

Moses Holms is a frame story. The author brilliantly uses the outer body experience as a method to extrapolate his intention to save a man's soul. One man's devotion to legacy, atonement and ultimate redemption of a deceased friend whose belief in demonic possession facilitated his demise and damnation to Sheol is truly remarkable. Within this frame, the reader is given an extensive view into the rites of exorcism through the eyes of heavenly warriors engaged in battle to save the soul of Moses Holms. Further, the reader views this frenzied struggle through the eyes of the victim, Moses himself, a completely novel approach to the process of exorcisms. Of course, the demons have their say and Lucifer and the apostate angels prove to be worthy opponents for Mikhail, Azrael and Zedkiel. But in the end, it is Moses who rebukes Satan, dies, but saves his soul. Good stuff.

In closing, four poems were also added which helped to form the book's format as each poem, precedes a short story and is thematically linked. "Smoky Mirrors and Devil's Dust" discusses a young girl's struggle to save herself from herself through the help of a mysterious "Queen" and a loving friend. "Rosa" is a poetic tribute to the mystery of a poor woman's unselfish love for a poor boy. "Cold Room", and insightful review of a chamber and its ever changing whimsical tenants, is alluring. Finally, there is "Kill Shot", a brief, powerful look into the power of black magic.

It is my sincerest hope that you have been informed enough to enjoy Woodbine and accept it for what it is – mostly truth, some fiction, but a joyful, albeit frightening, experience.

"Buck"

William "Buck" Godfrey

# TABLE OF CONTENTS

William "Buck" Godfrey

# THE COLD ROOM

There is a cold room at the end of the hallway.
In that room are memories
Of warm smiles, warm conversations,
Warm sunshine, warm blankets
And warm milk.
I raised a daughter in that room.
Her nickname was "Fats."
She was chubby and bowlegged and playful.
She loved her room,
Which was red and white.
The carpet was shaggy white.
The wallpaper, which I hung myself,
Was white, with red hearts interspersed.
The furniture was egg-shell white.
It was a beautiful, happy room.
Fats and I had fun in her room.
Then she grew up, tall and pretty
And went off to college.

Then the room became silent

Not long after, I scraped the
White wallpaper with the red hearts
Off the wall and painted it beige.
I gave the furniture – the egg-shell white dresser,
desk, chair, vanity,

And chest of drawers to a needy family.
The white carpet - so lush, so beautiful,
So warm, became plain, cold hardwood.
I sighed and closed the door
To the empty room.

Without my daughter, the room
At the end of the hall became
Cold and empty, and I cried.

In 2000, Nana arrived
To live in that room
Her Robert had passed
And our home became her home.
Although bed-ridden from old age and Arthur,
She was a delight.
She did not have teeth,
But fresh fried shrimp, bream, shell cracker And her
favorite, okra soup with 'shine bones," Stood no
chance against Nana's
Fast moving jaws and hardened gums. Something
"cold and sweet," – be it
Milkshakes, sweet tea or Coca Cola –
Completed the recourse.
It was said that she could not
Or would not talk.
However, in secret, special moments
She and I talked,
And she would smile, sometimes laugh.
Soon that room became warm again.
We took her everywhere
And a social being she was.
Some included these:
Rashan's and Colin's weddings
Where she had a ball.

## William "Buck" Godfrey

A banquet where she ate
Three different salads – one of which was hers.
Fishing at Charlie Elliot's,
She hated it.
Too much country.
Ms. Malcome's fish fry
Where she ate three complete dinners.
Piccadilly's at South Dekalb mall.
Later at the entrance,
She hung out in her wheelchair
Hat tilted, amused by the eccentric
Shenanigans of her people.
At home, she enjoyed visitors,
Especially those who brought
Folding money. Otherwise, she
And the daytime TV stories were inseparable.

Then one day,
Rainno and I hoisted Nana from her bed
To place her in the wheelchair.
Suddenly blood began to drip From both of her
bared feet.
"Lawdy! Lawdy! Lawdy!" she screamed.
From that room, she went to the hospital.
From the hospital, she went to the hospice.
Soon after, she passed quietly,
Without a sound.
So dignified. So ready.
At her funeral, I discovered why.
She looked brand new, like a bride
On her special day

She had gone to be with her Robert
In the land where the Woodbine twineth
And the sycamore ceased to bloom.

## William "Buck" Godfrey

The next morning, snow flakes fell
From a gray, melancholy sky.
It covered the windows of the room.
And the chill of death reigned supreme.
The room at the end of the hallway,
Once again, became empty and cold.

Five years passed.
The room was repainted lemon.
A king sized bed with a classy
Maroon and gold spread
Replaced the medical bed of my friend.
Nana's chest of drawers
And night table only remained.
Beautiful, off white custom made
Blinds completed the décor.

Now four cuddly tomboys –
Bailey, Gabrielle, Carter and Morgan
Romp and squeal and smile and cry
And sleep in that cold room.
Only now that room has a pulse
And warm sunshine enters and covers
Boo-ga-loo, Gabby, Scrappy and Commissioner.
Nana is proud. These are her great-grands.
It is said that Life is a circle.
For me, it came full bear

The cold room at the end of the hallway
Is now forever warm and vibrant
With Nana's lineage
Through Fats' and Colin's fruit.

*W.B.G.*

# ROSA

We had eaten red rice and fish,
But I was still hungry
So I wanted up for Rosa.
She had worked hard
In the rich man's kitchen
Since six o'clock that morning
And she would be tired and bent.
Her face would be dark and drawn
And her big eyes would water;
Her nose would run from the cold.
But she would smile when she saw me
And fire up the stove.

She would fry bacon
In the big black pan,
Throw in two eggs
Which she took from the icebox
And then mix it all together
With last night's rice.
We'd eat in silence
Then chase all that
With a steeping cup of hot postum.
We'd talk some.
Soon I'd leave her room
Feeling good and warm.

But Rosa didn't come home.
She missed the whole winter
And in the spring
I looked down at my friend
With the scent of roses and gladiolas
Choking me.
And I was glad
That I had loved her,
But I was pissed at the undertaker.
He had put too much powder
On her sad, beautiful face

*W.B.G.*

# THE WIDOW DART

Chance had brought Reece to Veredelict. It was early morning when he awoke and the train had long since stopped. In seven hours it had traveled an eternity. He had tried, not very hard, to find work in Luken and, as expected, had not been very successful. It is true that news, especially concerning the darker side of a person's character, travels fast in a village, but Reece's lack of employment was due far more to his natural aversion to work than to the upturned noses of the little old ladies of Luken.

On his last night there, Reece penny-pinched a bowl of soup and afterwards retired to an abandoned boxcar which two nights before had become his home. He nestled in a corner among the frost bitten and acrid smelling hay and soon fell into a deep sleep. He did not stir when the locomotive whistle sounded. He had just begun to snore when the chug-chug-chug of the train's engine signaled its departure from Luken. This was not a scheduled trip. There was no engineer visible in the cabin nor a coachman in the caboose. Fate and Destiny would be the signalmen who guided the way of the iron monster as it wended its way through the murky fog with its only passenger.

Reece stretched his aching muscles and rubbed his eyes. Dusting the hay from his clothes, he arose and peered through the slats of the boxcar. Reece was not a man of introspection, but the appearance of the country outside caused him to quaver slightly.

All was still. No breeze rustled the dead autumn leaves, and no birds flitted through the brush. No katydid chirped its seasonal love song. Most of the trees were dead, their once proud trunks blackened by moisture and decay. Others had toppled over completely, victims of the on-slaught of Time, and served as grim reminders of a stately grandeur long since passed. And present everywhere was the parasitic mistletoe. Even the few oaken stalwarts that remained were entwined in the mistletoe's deathlike embrace.

Before long, they too, would join the others in this terrestrial cemetery.

Shrugging off this momentary feeling of uneasiness, Reece jumped from the boxcar to the damp ground. With a week's beard on his ruddy face, his hat pulled down to the brim, and hands shoved deeply into the pockets of his baggy pants, Reece Page doggedly trudged toward the village of Veredilect.

No one was to be seen, but Reece was unperturbed. The cold, damp New England air chilled his bones and he made his way to the local tavern, where he ordered a mug of rum and beer and quickly guzzled it. He ordered another and made his way to a corner booth near the pot-bellied stove. For a few moments he just sat and allowed the powerful brew to take effect.

Before long, however, his thoughts were centered on his next meal, and more important, spending money. His last dollar would go for the drink.

Besides the bartender, there were four old fogeys standing at the bar. All were sinister looking men with hard features and an air of mysticism about them. All wore dark muslin coats and flop hats. Their trousers were of coarse wool and gray dust covered their heavy boots. All smoked pipes. Although each had a subtle individuality, they all had a oneness peculiar to and indicative of the village. Indeed, they seemed as interminable as Time itself, but taken out of their seemingly functional context of the village, Veredilect, they would vanish into an existence long since past, similar to the townsmen in Puritan Salem.

Reece had not noticed them. At the moment he was scanning the want ad section of the local newspaper. One advertisement caught his eye.

It read: **Wanted, Handyman. Free room and board (30-35), experienced. Contact the Widow Dart, Creek Road, Veredilect. Six week termination.**

Reece's spirit soared – "free room and board" – no heavy work. This was beyond belief.

9

He arose from the booth a little unsteadily and sauntered over to the bar where the old men stood. Reece asked aloud: "Can any one of you tell me how to get to Creek road?"

They turned in unison at the query from the heretofore silent stranger. Their grizzled, ashen faces gave Reece a start as they scrutinized him with quizzical and penetrating eyes. At last (and what seemed to be an eternity to Reece), the eldest spoke up in a rasping tone.

"So you're going to work for the Widow, are ye? Well, you're a likely candidate. Reckon she'll be glad to have you. It's about that time of the year again." And in the next breath he gave directions. "Walk east to the edge of the village and then turn due north. Her house is a brown three story on a hill. You can't miss it." With these final words, he turned to his buddies with a glint in his eye and continued his drinking.

The old man's words had struck something deep within Reece, but he was unable to fathom its underlying meaning. Although visibly shaken, he managed to reach into his pocket and pay for his drinks. He then rushed through the swinging doors of the tavern to the cobblestoned street, heading east toward the home of the Widow Dart.

By the time Reece rapped on the heavy door of the gabled dwelling, it was dusk. After some moments, he rapped again. This time the antique knob turned and the door was opened slowly and deliberately. A tall, gaunt woman in the garb of a domestic appeared. Her grim stare rendered Reece uneasy, but he managed to mutter his business and she implored him to enter. The great door creaked shut behind them, as if operated mechanically.

"You saw the ad in the paper?" she inquired. "Yes," replied Reece, visibly shaken. (How could she know his reason for coming?)

"You are the only applicant, but you'll do fine," she continued, matter of factly. "There is nothing much to do, but the Widow relishes her privacy. She is wealthy and a little eccentric. She insists on being left alone. You see, she had a tragedy some years back. Her fiancé…," she paused and cast her head downward. "She never quite got over it. It happened on her wedding day. Her anniversary will be coming soon, however. Then she will be happy once again." This last sentence she repeated as if she were entranced in some occult reverie.

"You are hired, if you want the job. It ends in six weeks. Tomorrow is September 13. Your time will start then. The job is better than most I'm sure you will agree."

Reece agreed. He had no choice. The job suited him. He could never be equal to a task involving intellectual endeavor or sustained labor. Anything menial, as long as it produced immediate results suited Reece. Besides, need necessitated it. He had nothing. He was led to his room, ecstatic but uneasy.

After some weeks, Reece became phobic, uneasy. At first, he had grown to enjoy his chores, which were simple enough. Clean floors, rake leaves, dust books and furniture. The tranquility of the place, the more than adequate room and board and the other pleasures afforded him were indeed desirable to this outcast of a man. But Reece wanted out.

Of late he had begun to have doubts, fears, and feelings of dread. For the past few nights while cleaning the hallways, Reece had heard mourning, a subdued cry of deepest sorrow. At other times he had smelled the aroma of cheap perfume which seemed to ooze from the walls and tapestries. Instead of intoxicating, it suffocated and rendered him nauseous. Yet the bearer of the mysterious odor was nowhere to be seen. He became more perplexed as each day passed and each night he would retire to his room, his mind full of anxieties. Sleep would come, but it was troubled, restless sleep. He would have fantastic dreams which added to his growing apprehensiveness.

Sometimes he was a frightened child futilely attempting to escape the grasps of a shrouded spectre. He would run and run and run but the spectre, as if floating on air, came closer and closer and closer. Just as it would reach out its long, sinewy hands to grab him, he would awaken – his heart pounding with fear and his clothes reeking with the odoriferous smell of nervous perspiration.

At other times he was a minister, dressed in black, reciting the eulogy at his own funeral. Even stranger was the fact that aside from himself, there was only one other person present in the chapel.

She was dressed in mourning and knelt quietly near the coffin, her head covered with a shroud. None of these, however, disturbed Reece as much as his last dream.

He was a passenger on a train heading nowhere. The grinding sounds of the wheels on the track and the rhythmic chug-chug-chug of the engine pierced the still night air and finally lulled him to sleep. When he awakened, he found that he was not alone in in his compartment.

There was someone or something there. From what he could discern, the figure was that of an old woman, her head covered and her face covered with a veil.

She sat motionless, erect – peering through the filmy window. There was a purpose of resolution, a sternness in her gaunt appearance that unnerved Reece completely. Perspiration streamed down his face, and his hands became cold and clammy. All of a sudden the train lurched forward and was immersed in total blackness as if it had plunged into the bowels of the earth itself. No light was to be seen, but the shrouded figure of the woman remained motionless.

Then came the odor, the suffocating malodorous odor of the strange perfume. Reece began to gasp for air. He lunged forward and tugged at the windows, but they were locked from the outside. He raced for the door, but it too was locked. There was no escape.

Just at that moment the woman arose – slowly and resolutely. Reece slinked over to a corner of the compartment almost delirious with fear. She slowly came toward him, step by step. She threw off her shroud and...he would awaken – sick with fear and apprehension. As he lay there on his cot, Reece realized that something must be done. Otherwise, he would go insane.

The six weeks were almost up and surprisingly enough, he had never seen the Widow Dart. The proclamation of his duties had come through the mouth of the tall, gaunt overseer. She, through his eyes, must be the owner, and the Widow Dart only a myth. And yet he would hear two voices at night after supper. One was the gruff but nasal voice of the overseer and the other which had to be the mysterious widow was throaty and guttural, but feminine. This was strange indeed, and Reece had resolved himself to find a solution.

One evening around dusk, Reece crept silently from his room. His destination was a singular chamber located at the extreme end of the hallway. This was the private dining area and the room from which the two distinct voices were audible.

Upon nearing the room, he saw a form disappear behind the purple curtains. This happened in an instant, but Reece was sure that the figure was female and was garbed in a bridal gown. This was indeed not the overseer. Was it the mythical Widow? Reece could hold his curiosity in check no longer. With a few quick steps and a lunge, he drew the curtains open.

14

Nothing! There was absolutely nothing! Only a flicker of a candle in the room indicated any kind of movement. It had gone, vanished! Only the smell of the suffocating perfume lingered, the suffocating perfume of the dream. Reece retreated, but the grating sound of a door being opened at the far end of the chamber rendered him motionless. He was sick with fear.

Suddenly, as if by some mysterious force, he moved, entranced. Step by step he drew towards the now fully opened door. The odor of the suffocating perfume engulfed him, overwhelmed him. Loud cacophonous music from a pipe organ blared, deafening Reece. Shadows from a thousand flickering candles performed a macabre dance on the ebony walls. He entered the compartment and then the door closed behind him.

Something took a firm grip on his arm and held him securely. He was visibly shaking when the slumped over figure appeared beside him. The smell of the perfume pervaded the air. He was choking. Some murmuring was heard and the "nuptials" were completed. Reece could now kiss the bride. The organ built to a high pitched crescendo as Reece, half delirious raised the veil of his new bride. He glared like a madman in to the bulbous, watery eyes of the decadent, pallid face of the Widow. He leaned backward violently, but was entwined in her long, sinewy arms like the oaks in the choking grip of the mistletoe. It was an embrace of death in a union most unnatural.

In the distance a bell knelled. In the tavern at Veredilect, the eldest of the four fogeys read aloud from the Want-ad section of the paper.

**Wanted, Handyman. Free room and board.(30-35), experienced. Contact the Widow Dart,Creek Road, Veredilect. Six week termination.**

The paper was dated October 24. The old man looked at his friends with a glint in his eye and continued drinking.

# KILL SHOT

When one kills a man,
He, in a flash, obliterates
That man's present and future.

When one hurts a child,
He voids the child's present
And limits the child's future.

When a man mistreats a woman,
He diminishes his past,
He negates his present,
And fast forwards his future
To the wiles of a baleful
fate.
"Mr., you shouldn' o' done dat!"
"Whatchu gon' do, ol hag?" the big man
bellowed.
"You okay, Lucy? Um gon get some ice."
"Mr., you gon' pay," Lucy warned.
"Let's go, Joe. It's late."
Joe cussed, and spat and
left.
This was hog killin' time,

William "Buck" Godfrey


And Joe killed hogs.

April came in vibrant
beauty.
Sparrows chirped in oak
trees,
Honeybees and butterflies
Competed for nectar
In the succulent sunflower patch.

At the Fielding's Funeral
Parlor
The smell of gladiolas
And red roses filled the air.
Someone had died.
Above the hushed
Murmuring
Of the gathered few
Were the words of Lucy's
Friends.
"He only weigh sixty pound."
"Shouldn' 'a' cuss Lucy."
"Shouldn' 'a' touch her neither."

"Umm! Umm! Umm!"
"Ain't sayin' nuthin neither."


*W.B.G.*

# THE WATCHER AT CUT BRIDGE ROAD

Two miles down Cut Bridge Road (follow the right fork) on the left lived most of my James Island cousins. All the land up to the old airport cross the three fields to Road 11, approximately thirty-five acres belonged to the Smiths and the Slaters. The property had been inherited from Samson Duckson whom no one cared to discuss. But that's okay. All my relatives had homes here with the exception of my cousins Catherine and Bertha who lived on another part of James Island and Lulie, Linda, and Harold who had moved to the New York City in the 40's and 50's.

The lay of the property seemed calculated, designed. My Aunt Hester's cottage had a vantage point whereby she could observe any and everything. To her right on a 45 degree angle stood Lizzie's fine cinder block house. Almost directly in front of Hester's cottage, some fifty yards away, resided Helen and her family in a white and burgundy framed cottage. To Helen's right, catty corner, rose

Aunt Willa's beige and brown knotty pine cottage and about forty yards to the right of Aunt Willa, resided Anna and Julius. Their home, a two-storied red brick and cedar modern, was attractive because it was new and unique with its glossy white paint and Dutch roofing. All came to bare, however, under the watchful, scrutinizing and sometimes baleful eye of my Aunt Hester.

It became evident that Hester became matriarch by proxy. No one knew if she were the eldest of her sisters: Pauline, Willa, or Big Vi.

These three had birth certificates. Hester had none. But more than any one fact, my Aunt had the "power", the "thing" and no one, I mean no one, trifled or toyed with it. "I like Willa, but I love Hester!" My grandmother would say. I never understood this as a youngster. Later I learned what her utterance meant.

The family was a sizeable one. Other than Big Vi, who was childless, Hester's sisters produced the bulk. Aunt Willa gave birth to Helen, Bertha, Lizzie, Catherine, Lulie, Linda and two boys – Harold and Jackie. Helen was the eldest; Linda was the youngest. Pauline, my grandmother, conceived Octavia, my Mom, Thelma, my aunt, and my uncles, Dan and George. Aunt Hester bore Anna early and Ash late. So late that at age one, Ash became the uncle of Anna's son Corey, aged nineteen. Needless to say, this was "hush humor" at its finest.

The Smiths and Slaters loved each other and got along fairly well. No one wanted for anything. Sharing and caring were practiced family values. Plus, they lived and worked on a farm. So the Smiths and Slaters were almost self-sufficient.

Other than Bertha, who suffered from the ill effects of diabetes, these women were physically and mentally strong. Each could outwork any one man, whip most and outsmart the rest. All had a role to play and they did it well. But all deferred to Hester in matters that required guile, scope or toughness.

After all, it was Aunt Hester whom the doctors at "colored" Roper Hospital determined was so close to death that they placed her in a room next to the morgue Six weeks later, this same Hester slipped out the hospital and walked the ten miles to Cut Bridge Road and home. The family only knew she had returned when they saw smoke puffing from the chimney of her cottage and smelled the aroma of cornbread pervading the air. And she never mentioned this incident once and no one asked.

This Hester could be intimidating, not so

much by "big woman" presence, but by her eyes. Her left eye was the brightest hazel; her right eye could be slate gray or stygian black depending upon a given situation. These were piercing eyes that reached inside a person and rendered him uneasy, fearful without knowing why. And she rarely spoke. She only stared.

There were times when she attended the many socials near her place. When the revelers sighted my Aunt approaching, a kind of uncomfortable hush settled. All gave deference to the woman with the "power" and the strange eyes. It is said that the hardest drinkers sobered, "good time" women became nuns and crap shooters pocketed their bones. It was understood that Aunt Hester came to the crowd. Never, in more than three decades, did she give a hint of being with the crowd. No! And always, right at dusk, she retraced her path through the field to perch at her unvarying watch in the front window of her cottage. No goodbyes, no farewells, no ta tas. Nothing more, nothing less, nothing else.

From the window Hester saw Gene, a bright skinned fellow from New York City smooth Lizzie's ruffled feathers with his slick talk and sharp dressing so much so, that she allowed that "do nothin" to stay with her and play the common law game. Lizzie even followed him to Harlem and when she returned to James Island, she spoke a "new" language – hip, jive and sadly imitated. She spoke a New

York brogue, but with a James Island Geechie enunciation. Lizzie sounded foolish. Some liked it; others ignored it; Hester hated it, especially when Lizzie put on "airs" while she spoke.

The last time she left to go up North would be her last. This time she returned and seemed more like herself. She spoke less and less like a Harlemite and more and more like a James Islander. Everyone liked it, including Hester, especially since Gene elected to stay in New York.

When men cheated on their wives, the "Watcher" knew. With the wife asleep, they would sneak away, put the car in neutral and push it to Cut Bridge Road. About 100 yards down the road, they would jump in and crank the car – no headlights – until they felt a safe distance from the house. Then they would switch on the lights, close the door of the car and head for whiskey breath, sticky fondlings and whore funk. The deed done, they would reverse the game plan and secretly and silently slip in bed with the still sleeping wife. Hester did not like these "sorry excuses for men."

When Big Silo paid the price of fornication in Charleston, she heard his death screams, fifteen miles away. Nish finally had enough and tied him drunk and naked to the four posts of their bed.

She took her time and boiled a big pot of

grits and potash. When the brew became good and hot and sticky, she awakened her sneaking "playboy".

She said, with pot in hand, bubbling over his naked privates, "Well plumber, yester night you laid your last pipe. Have some breakfast!" Here she poured the contents of the pot on the exposed crotch of Silo.

"Oh, Lawd! Good God! Oh, Lawd! Help me!" the man screamed. The pain was so intense that he broke the bed, bust through the windows and fell dead on the porch.

Miles away, Hester mumbled in Geechie, "Ain't no Dewine help here, broza. All dem gals you been wit'? Hot? Ain't ee, big boy. Lawd, dah man done broke dah bed, dah do' and fall dead on dah po'ch! Nish done sen' Silo t' see Ol' Scratch!" Hester smiled and put some logs inside the door of the stove.

Then, her voice boomed loud as she closed the door to the stove on the crackling fire: "Told Gloria fah stay home. I heah ee head bus' shrough dah win'shiel' o' dat crazy boy "Tub" ca', an' now ee rollin' fifty ya'd down Cut Bridge an' gon settle een dah ditch by dah a'po't, all bloody an' swole. D'a's 'bout twenny five done speed roun' Dead Man Curve! Ol' Scratch, you busy dis night. An' yo' oak tree at dah curve still ain't even got a scratch."

24

She laughed deliriously, shouting, "Dey won't listen 'bout the curve an' dah tree, but Scratch – he just smile wit' ee sh'ap teeth an' countin' book." Then she became pensive.

"Tol' Gloria tah stay home! Too late now. Too late!"

Next morning, the December mist creeped grim and gray over a scene of highway patrol cars with lights blinking, officers huddling and searching and the Death Wagon parked like a black vulture on one side of Cut Bridge Road.

"Here's the head!" a young patrolman hollered. "My God! She didn't have a chance."

Two men jumped from the Death Wagon and both half trotted to where the patrolman yelled. A serious looking fellow, slightly built jumped into the ditch and gently placed the head into a dark, cushioned bag being extremely careful not to allow any seepage to penetrate through the thick towel on to himself. He passed the bag to his partner, a big fellow with massive upper torso muscles, who carried it to the Death Wagon (coroner's van).

"Well, we're pretty much done here," the sergeant interjected. "All the ID is in the car. We'll notify the families."

"Two more," continued another officer speaking morosely to his fellow patrolmen while examining the base of the killer oak. "How long will it take for people to understand that this curve and this tree aren't going anywhere. And this tree has probably been here 200 years."

"Let's go!" called the sergeant. "The Fire Department's gotta wash the road down. Don't want anyone seeing this mess!" They slowly drove off.

Meanwhile, Anna's husband, Julius, sat in a rocking chair lazily puffing on the stogie that he always seemed to have in the right side of his mouth. A quiet, easygoing fellow, he just never seemed to "fit in" with the family. He was polite, friendly and even went to church on Sundays, but he could never be more than an outsider.

What really hurt him, especially with the men, was their unfounded and false knowledge that he was henpecked. It was said that Anna, six feet tall double jointed, with a six inch straight razor scar that extended from her left ear to the her lower jaw, ran the roost. It is said that she would, on occasion, just kick him square in the ass to see what would happen. Nothing ever did. It is also said that Julius would avoid any physical confrontation with her. She had actually beaten him – with her fists – on two separate occasions. Yessir! Yep.

She called the shots and made him "tow the line." As T K Smith said, "Uf dat 200 poun' 'oman tell 'im tah jump, he wouldn' evun as' how high. He would sta't tah jump!" And boy would they laugh till their eyes reddened and their bellies hurt.

But all this was hearsay, innuendo. Julius knew what they said and never responded. These men, except Bill, did not like the fact that he had finished high school, dressed neatly at all times and chose not to carouse with them. That was all. How they viewed him did not matter.

The truth is Julius ran things, maybe too much so. He loved Anna but Anna did not love him back. She was incapable of truly loving him as a typical wife. First, she was emotionally immature and this rendered her incapable of loving a good man. Second, she was trifling. After all, she exhibited no sophistication in speech, demeanor or refinement that would enhance the slightest spark of a meaningful relationship. In fine, the marriage was bestial, pure, unadulterated physical attraction.

And so he sat and rocked and thought of Anna's big hips, full breasts and smooth, mariny complexion. She had become his double jointed wild stallion that he rode with joy and abandon. That is until 3:00 this morning when she came home, climbed the steps, undressed and lay beside him smelling of moonshine, cigarette smoke and stinky sweat. This he would not condone. Angrily, he clenched his fists, and fell into a troubled sleep.

Julius snuffed his stogie and entered the house. He walked up the steps to the master bedroom. He opened the door and discovered that Anna had awakened and gone to the restroom. He reached under the king sized mattress and pulled out a strop. Then he sat on the bed, the strop across his lap. Dressed in a beautiful scarlet robe, Anna appeared from the bathroom. Her eyes, a bit pink from last night's activity, warmed when she saw Julius, then turned fearful when she saw the strop.

"Good morning," Julius spoke half-heartedly. "Sit please."

Anna mumbled, "Mawnin Julius," as she sat in the Lay-z-Boy.

"Good time last night and this morning?" Julius asked flippantly.

"Da bes'. Me an' da girls had a ball," she replied.

"What time did you get in?" Julius questioned.

"Around 3:00, I guess. Wha's all this

about? Ain't like I been out wit' no man!" Anna spoke strongly.

"Man? James Island doesn't have any men,"

"Well, at least the boys on James Island (sarcastically) know how to go out and have a good time! You can't expect me to jus' sit around all da time. You won't take me nowhere!"

"Don't raise your voice at me, woman! My rule is 12:00 curfew. After 12:00 is devil time." Julius became angry and stood. But this time Anna stood also.

"Um not takin' no mo' licking from that strop. No sir. I broke yo' rule and I'm sorry, but if you hit me wit' da strop, ee gon' be hell in here!" cried Anna.

"Now you got it comin. You'll remember the next time you come in my house after 12:00! Listening to those whorish cousins of yours. I'm gon beat it out ya."

And they went at it. For the better part of fifteen minutes, they fought and they fought. Julius had bit off more than he could chew as the saying goes. Anna used every fiber of her body to whip this man. She kicked, punched, bit, and scratched. Finally, just as some of the family members showed, Julius punched Anna in the mouth and she fell. She didn't stay down though. She ran from the bedroom down the stairs straight down the path to her Momma's house.

Julius – disheveled, scratched, bitten, embarrassed – stood helplessly facing the shocked and disgusted family who had tolerated him. Now they just shook their heads and walked away. Total and silent isolation froze him in time and space.

"You doesn't haffa say nut'n," Hester consoled. "We (Dantalion and Gap – wolf dog familiars) Ash and Corey heard an' saw ebbyting. You go to da pump, here's a rag, and clean yo' mout'. We gon see bout Mr.Julius!" Hester hissed.

"Now ya'll come ya. Dantalion an' Gap, ya'll lead. Go een da wood where Scratch walk two days 'fo' dah' full moon. Bring dese back: bat's wing, death head moth's wing, a crow eye, a sow's blood, a bullfrog's foot, shree lamb's ears, a squirrel's ear and a moccasin's head. Bring um fo' midnight."

She stooped down and hugged her dogs which she conjured from the secret cellar under her cottage. "Ya'll know my thoughts; ya'll know my thoughts; ya'll know where to go. Now run like da wind, but bring my boys back safe!" She kissed both of them and they both wagged their tails and growled in agreement.

"Ya'll boys follow as close as ya can, now. Ain't too bad. Now run like da wind!"

The back door pushed open, the two familiars and Ash and Corey left.

Hester, all business now, threw more logs in the stove. She reached in the corner and pulled out a good sized cauldron and placed it by the stove. "Lemme see now," she began thinking aloud. "I got some dried blackberry leafs, star of Bethlehem, tree tobacco an' nerum oleander." Hester's gray eye glowered in the light of the wood stove. She was on a mission. She called to Anna, examined her face and put her to bed just like she was four years old again. Julius had headed toward Cut Bridge Road in his pickup and no one noticed.

At 10:00 p.m. Dantalion and Gap returned. Hester muttered to them and patted their heads. She took them outside, fed and watered them and commanded them by sign to leave, and they disappeared through a door, camouflaged from view, back to the secret cellar. Soon after, Ash and Corey entered the front room only Ash and Corey had become humanoids. Both carried what Hester had requested in medium sized croaker sacks.

"Good, my boys. Good!" Hester smiled

broadly. "Ya'll eat dat cornbread and buttermilk I got fa ya ova dey." Then she looked at the humanoids and spoke to them in Latin: "Redirez ad tristinum a capite ad caleem."

Shortly, Ash and Corey became human again. "Go to bed when ya done."

"Yes, ma'am," they responded.

When everyone fell asleep, Aunt Hester went to work. She placed the cauldron on the hot stove and poured ingredients from six different vials in it. Next, she added water and brought the mixture to a boil. Then one by one she added the list of items from the croaker sack, continually stirring, clockwise, then counter-clockwise. Over each addition, she said aloud: "Morte – an alu bar anaba! Rise Grim Reaper and grab Julius!" The last plant to enter the cauldron was the nerum oleander. At this point, she hissed in that funny way and the gray eye became black and she repeated, "Morte to Julius! Morte to Julius! Morte to Julius! Six times. Only then did she stop stirring to let the cauldron cool. She sat down exhausted and slept with one eye open, the hazel eye.

Before sunrise, Hester trudged toward Anna's and Julius's house. In her right arm she carried a red pouch with black strings. It contained the ingredients from the cauldron.

The combination of herbs, plants, animal parts and conjuration would engage the nether world of Scratch and the Reaper to exact revenge on Julius.

She stopped at the clothesline and took a pair of Julius's boxer shorts and a tee shirt. Opening the door and climbing the steps, she entered the master bedroom. She laid the pouch, the shorts and the tee on a chair and pulled the mattress with bed-clothes attached to the side. Then she returned to the chair.

She placed each item on the floor and sat. In her lap, she first placed the boxer shorts, then the pouch and finally the tee shirt. She said some words from one of the Psalms and retrieved a needle and black thread from her skirt pocket.

Skillfully, she sewed the three items into one. When she had completed her work, it closely resembled a pentagram. She smiled grimly and returned to the bed.

She placed the pentagram on the right upper side of the box spring where Julius would lay. And she secured it with her handy needle and thread. Next, she pulled the bed clothes from the mattress and lay them to the side. Carefully, she lifted and positioned the mattress so it would look undisturbed and natural. She then placed her clenched right fist on the spot over the pentagram and said aloud: "In crucio requiescat!"

Hester now cleaned the room. When she had finished, there was no evidence of any fighting or ill feelings. She washed and dried the bedclothes, remade the bed and sprinkled the spread with hyssop and wolfbane. "Ha, ha, ha! What a combination." she laughed.

When she had finished, she literally patted herself on the back. The master bedroom was again a bridal chamber.

The sun began to glimmer in the East. She went to the closet and took a small suitcase. In it she placed all the necessaries that Anna would need for a week. She stopped at the door and looked around. Everything looked to be in place. She walked down the steps, negotiated the trail and entered her home.

Julius returned Sunday evening. He did not expect to see Anna or anyone. He parked the pickup and went upstairs to the bedroom. Boy was he surprised and relieved. The beautifully cleaned room gave him hope of a reunion with Anna. But alas, the man was bone tired and had to work tomorrow, Tuesday and Wednesday.

He took off his clothes, showered and put on his pajamas. He slipped under the fresh smelling herbal covers and slept like a dead man.

Wednesday came and went and Julius' pickup had not moved. Hester talked to Gap in the dark enumerating Julius' last dreams in a cold, detached obloquy.

"On Monday, dah the Reaper sta't up the dah steps from dah grave Simon dug. But ee didn' reach dah top - six steps sho't. Nex' day dah Reaper an' Scratch almos' reach dah top- Shree step sho't. Wensdy, dah root took hol' o' dah fella body. Itchin' stingin' - all ovah an' ee can' move. Dah pain in ee neck, shoulda', belly, privates, legs an' foots become a heby burden. The cold heaviness of intense suffering crushed him as the Reaper and Scratch made it to da top. Go get Dantalion. We going to get the coction from da mattress an' bury it where Scratch walk." She finished and the three of them went to Julius's house.

The next morning, the gray coroner's van with the help of the slightly built man and the big fella transported Julius's body to the morgue. And surveying and leering over all was Hester, the Watcher of Cut Bridge Road.

William "Buck" Godfrey

# SMOKY MIRRORS AND DEVILS' DUST

Can you live with your loneliness?
Can you accept a future without children?
Can you expect the unexpected to be
expected?
Can you love yourself selfishly?

She listens, but will not hear. She observes,
but will not see. She feels, but will not
respond. She needs, but will not inquire.

Not long after, she began her odyssey. She
wanted to discover who she was. What she had
accepted was the hollow Image reflected by
the frail
Mirror of her mind –
Made tangible by the clouded glass In her
woman room.
At best, it was worst, but she chose.
Confused and confined in the mockery Of a
Culture which fosters
And forces the sense of having to

Belong, Now!

She fervently began to search, to emulate,
To lie. Please – Oh, please! Love?
It don't love nobody.
Survive, stress, work, live?
Die!

Driven by the inner struggle to be,
Caught in the ebb tide of Time,
She joined the caravan of dusty, Hollow, dying
wind-strewn maidens
Who fruitlessly search for the right to be.

So like them, she began to merchandise
Herself. She held auctions of
Irreplaceable parts of her private garden
Sold to the bidder who was as
Impotent and hollow as she

SHE DID NOT REALIZE THAT
SHE WAS THE HONEY IN THE BELLY OF A LION

Frustrated, she vigorously began
To follow a new path.
She sipped Pink Ladies at Blue Light Clubs,
And listened to empty words
Emanating from equally empty men
Dressed in expensive Sean John's
That reeked of whore sweat and cheap
cologne.
After many nights of blue smoke
And slimy floors and hollow talk,
She succumbed to empty feelings
And gave herself to empty trysts –

William "Buck" Godfrey

All numb, all insenate, all dead.
After so many attempts
At such a frenzied pace,
She fell silently to the ground.

Immediately and maggot like –
Her soul, long tormented and disgraced,
Pushed rigorously against her skin,
Struggling to free itself from this
Rotting entombment, to fly
To the permanence of the shadow land.

With baited breath, I ran to where she lay
Prone and naked to the world.
She gasped and her chest heaved.
Like the soul, Life was leaving.
It, too had had its share of failure
And frustration and abuse.
It sought the refuge of the grave.

But I breathed into her mouth –
Slowly, carefully, rhythmically.
After many frantic minutes,
Her chest rose and fell by itself,
Much like a babe at rest
In the security and comfort of its crib.

Then her soul, defiant in defeat,
Groaned aloud and like a demon, Cursed me.
I cradled my friend in my arms And took her to
Queen Esther's House of Bones.
She had told me she loved me.
But I only saw her tears
And pitied her feelings.

William "Buck" Godfrey

Two months passed. Late one night
The phone rang. It was Queen Esther.
"Call her. Call her now," she whispered.

I dialed her number.
On the third ring, she picked up.
"Hi," I said. "Meet me at the shop at 6:30."
"I'll be there," she sounded relieved.

I saw her park her car and opened the door.
When she entered the shop,
Our eyes met transfixed.
Nothing was said; the place was silent,
Life seemed suspended and
She was beautiful –
Maybe sadder but wiser, but beautiful!
The cream colored pant suit she wore
With the scarlet scarf around her neck
Enhanced her bronze, flawless
Complexion and clear brown eyes.

She came directly to the table
Where I anxiously awaited
Then stood to greet her.
She sat and smiled warmly,
Then gently touched my hand.
She spoke thusly:
I heard your frantic steps when I fell.
I saw the panic in your eyes.
I felt your lips on mine

As they blew life into my lungs.
I trembled when you lifted me
And carried me to the Queen.

I listened as you told my story,
I wanted to thank you so much
But I had no strength and slept.

When I awakened, I called your name.
The Queen came and gave me Tiswin To drink.

Again, I slept,
This time, I dreamed.
I dreamt that you were lonely
So I told you that I loved you.
Circumstances forbade such a love.
"I never loved," you said. And walked away.
I did not know how to handle this
And had no one to explain
So I asked the Queen. She replied:
Go grab your friend who brought You.
In him you will find
John Donne's Valediction Forbidding Mourning.
You have grown
And wisdom awaits you.
He will take your burning heart
And eat it like the Host.
You both will gain perpetual
Nourishment because the
Flame is eternal and provides.

"He, not understand love?" she mocked.
He truly understands
Because he has experienced pain,
He will keep you and protect
You and set you free.
No one can conquer the world.

No one can make another love
When the object is not love.
Travel the boulevards and streets
That you know. he will be there.
Be mindful of this as you leave
This place. You are a lady,
"The honey in a belly of the lion."
And she walked away.

All of this she related and
Empathized with my plight.
She knew me, I knew her.
We had been in love since Genesis.
I ordered her favorite – White hot chocolate.
We smiled a genuine smile
At each other, and held hands.
"When you go home, look in the
Mirror of your woman room.
Then you will find the princess/Queen.
And the figure at your side is me.

*W.B.G.*

# THE STRANGE CASE OF MOSES HOLMS

## 1.

He lay peacefully, finally. Death had taken the hump from his bent back and Death had removed the embarrassing bulge that protruded from his scrotum like an unwanted appendage. This deformity added to the specter that his hunched back supported a heavy weight without the support of his legs. His appearance rendered him caricature-like which, at a given moment, could topple over from the strain of keeping itself vertical.

Death had also permanently allayed the chronic and excruciating arthritic pain which Mr. Moses had endured without complaint over two decades. Through observation, this had made walking a chore and just merely standing to walk a major endeavor. Also vanished, again, thanks to Death, was his muted fear of the Root which unrelentingly toyed and jabbed with the man's physical, social, and mental well-being. He firmly believed that he was constantly under assault by demons and sprites-emissaries of Beezlebub, which could appear in any form and do him harm. This thought alone kept him wary of anything unfamiliar, especially strangers.

Paradoxically then, Death ministered to Mr.Moses as a kindly hospice physician and caregiver. It had relieved him of all worldly pain and worries. More importantly, through transition, he had regained the essence of who he was in early life – a man: kind, fearless, and free. And Billy, a mortician and one of the regulars at Dunkin, would see to the rest.

The coffee shop, an afternoon / evening meeting place for a motley crew of truckers, mechanics, hunters, painters, roofers, ex-army and biblical experts, had closed for repairs the second week in January. Consequently, Mr. Moses had no place to socialize, to hang out, and to be with friends away from his home where he could temporarily escape the personal demons that plagued him. Somewhat surprisingly, he stubbornly refused Hiram's offer to drive him to the Burger King where his cronies had relocated. No one questioned why. That was simply Mr. Moses' way.

Meanwhile, the Randi, during the closing, called his home on a daily basis. Each time he had cheerfully answered. In fact, I believe he looked forward to her calls. Speaking with the Randi uplifted him, made him embrace hope, gave him a purpose in spite of the groaning and growling of the malicious imps in his head.

On Valentine's Day, they spoke as two Platonic lovers – she, neutered by an outdated culture – he, trapped in his deformity, hoping beyond the nirvana of a pipedream, to experience real love and its nuances with her. Conversely, although the Randi "had feelings" for Mr. Moses, she had resigned herself to the lonely life of celibacy imposed upon widowed Hindu women. It was complete and final. Unknown to Mr. Moses, she had accepted her fate as it was. The giving of her virtue, especially to a "foreigner", would be a bane to herself, her family, and centuries of careful devotion to Krishna.

Further, she had learned the art of survival from the others of her kind who had come to America, poor and destitute. More sinister, the Randi had been trained by the White-Eye capitalist to suppress the emotion of the heart and, instead, follow the cold logic of the mind. Consequently, she used her station in life as both a boon and a bastion. She would give just enough of herself to extract money for her needs. If it came to a choice of giving totally of herself, she would retreat and withdraw into the secure confines of her "culture". Chicanery with impunity!

And so, with nothing to lose and everything to gain, she played the game.

When her shift ended, she would wash her hands and head straight to Mr. Moses' table. She sat close to him and engaged him in small talk. Then she gently touched his hands like a dog lover fondling a puppy. At long last, the charade would end with a school girl's kiss on the cheek. "Mr. Mos" as she referred to him in broken English, literally glowed with a reserved delight – he so long without female companionship, he who mutely was trying to understand these new feelings that both excited him and made him wary. He thanked her with a smiling nod and slipped her an envelope of dead Presidents, this in plain sight of anyone present. He had money and she needed money.

This was no one's business but his own. After all, he had financially helped quite a few of those who frowned on this. So he continued his kindness to the Randi without the slightest hint of guilt or embarrassment.

On February 15, the phone at Mr. Moses' went unanswered. The next morning early, the Randi called. Still, there was no response. In a panic, she called the Death Angel, he who seemed to know everything about anything; especially the Bible and information concerning those who may be sick or those who hovered near death. As soon as he heard about Mr. Moses, he hesitated. He had tried a year or so earlier to bilk the man into giving him Power of Attorney in a scam that was thwarted by Sam,

Jamal and three other regulars. Mr. Moses had taken ill and before he knew what happened, the Death Angel was on the verge of having him declared mentally unstable. Accordingly, he would minister his affairs and eventually profit from the "kindness" as a caretaker.

After some thought, he realized that he must go. He and Mr. Moses were "friends" despite of what had happened. The Death Angel jumped into his truck, cranked it, and drove to Mr. Moses'. Upon arrival, he jumped from the cab of the truck and walked around the house. Nothing seemed amiss. He then knocked on the door a few times calling Mr. Moses' name as he did so. No answer. He tried the doorknob which was locked. For good measure, he knocked on the door harder than before. Still, there was no response. Mr. Moses was eccentric and sometimes just wanted to be left alone. This Death Angel surmised and gave it no further thought. Neither did he return the Randi's call. Whether he did this by design or merely forgot would be pure conjecture. He jumped in his truck, cranked it, and drove to his home.

With no response from the Death Angel, the Randi became more frantic than before. This time she called Hiram who probably knew Mr. Moses as well or better than anyone at the shop. After calming her down and giving her some reassurance, he jumped in his red pickup and drove to Mr. Moses' place. When he arrived, he checked everything thoroughly even attempting to see through a rip or tear in the black, Hefty trash bags Mr. Moses used to cover his window to ward off the evil of the Root. Hiram banged on the door with his calloused fists. He knew Mr. Moses would open the door for him or at least respond. After he called his name five or six times, he felt that something was amiss. He repeated his efforts, but like before, there was no response. Hiram immediately dialed 911 on his cell phone. The Emergency Response team came and found Moses Holms dead.

Within the next couple of hours, Mr. Moses' body would be transported to the morgue where he literally "lay on ice" for nearly a month. His siblings, two brothers and a sister, denied his existence. During this interim, no other family came forth. Accordingly, Mr. Moses' body remained unclaimed. About midway through the second week in March, after the authorities had exhausted all lawful inquiries, his remains were transported to Billy's. To all of his friends this was a welcome relief. Each in his own way felt some vindication, some closure to this sad affair. Now Mr. Moses could be funeralized and buried by someone familiar.

2.

On the day of the funeral, I had arrived early. For some unknown reason, I wanted to be the first to see if he looked all right. Was he okay? Did he need a friend? Deep in my heart of hearts, I could always feel Mr. Moses' loneliness, his alienation. Even when he joked with the guys, when he laughed at one of Darryl's wisecracks, he always seemed alone, isolated as though the seat he occupied in the center of the shop was a kind of bastion and its sole inhabitant remained constantly on guard. The man was kind, loving and even affable, but although he was with the guys, he was not one of the guys. Hence, the name Mr. Moses, not Moses or Mo', was used as a sign of respect for privacy and dignity. And so, I sat alone in the small, cold room peering at his statuesque profile lying rigid and still in the state–issued, charcoal gray, pine box with one flat opening for his face. My thoughts ranged from anger to relief, from pity to elation. No one knew that his remains had been sent to another mortuary.

The director there had ordered him to be cremated. I called this man and asked for a meeting stating emphatically that Mr. Moses had friends. Rather than meet, knowing that cremation wasn't an option, he returned the body to the state. I guess he figured that whatever money the authorities would pay wasn't worth what he would face. The mortuary was a large one whose clientele would not include a Moses Holms.

Soon, Billy, dressed neatly, but somberly in a funeral gray suit, neatly pressed and spotless white shirt and a matching silver silk tie, entered. He nodded at me and smiled like only a mortician can – comforting, reassuring, caring. Then he quietly walked the few steps to where Mr. Moses lay and leaned to look into the pine box. Billy's demeanor was much like that of an art connoisseur admiring a fine piece of work. Then he spoke.

"Looks good, don't he? Looks like he's finally sleeping well. Sharp lookin' guy all spruced up!" Billy's faced glowed and after a pause, he continued, this time looking directly at me.

"I know you know, but a lot of people don't know that after the actual body dies, the hair and nails keep growing for a spell. Truth be told, as the skin dries, it pulls back making hair and nails seem longer. Not so here. Moses' skin stayed strangely moist for a good while, then shrunk."

At this juncture, he returned his gaze to the pauper's box and added animatedly, "Boy, he had a lot o' hair! Nails longer than my pinky. Our people gave him a good haircut and shave. Nails manicured nicely too. Glad he came to us. We family, you know. Man, he looks good!"

Billy stopped and looked at me for approval. I nodded and forced a smile of agreement.

In a serious vein he intoned, "Shame, the way nobody claimed him, shame! And he was such a nice man. Never a frown; never an unkind word. Took care of a lot o' people at Dunkin. Especially Country. Had a brown bag of food every day for him. Shame!" He was bitter now. "But they gon' pay! The relatives, I mean. They gon' pay to the Man. He got a two edged sword."

He looked my way again. I could tell her had choked up, but Billy, as was his wont, gathered himself and spoke casually, matter of factly.

"I gave him one of my blue suits and this maroon tie. Bought him a nice shirt and underwear too." And repeating again, "Boy, he looks good; good enough to go for a job interview! Oh. He left something for you. Was in the big leather shoulder bag he carried. An envelope or something. Had 'Coach' written on the front. I'll give it to you."

That said, he looked away from Mr. Moses' body to me and chuckled. "I'll see you later", he concluded. Then he turned and meandered down the hallway – shoulders

stooped, shuffling gait: "The oldest seventy –
four year old known to mankind!" we joked at
the shop.

I loved the guy. Everyone did. Billy was
just a genuinely nice, likeable guy who minded
his business and always seemed to smile. He
never raised his voice and seemed positive
about everything. Besides that, he was a
gentleman of the first order. Unassuming and
cordial, Billy was everyone's friend.

Alone once again in the death room, my
mind began to struggle with one of Life's great
puzzles. How could this seemingly kind man be
dealt such an unlucky hand in a game that he
seemed to have mastered. He was totally
independent. He asked for nothing and spoke
his mind, and that very rarely. He had money
and he had health, but in the end he had been
treated cruelly, rudely and disrespectfully by
the mere human condition of trying to live life
as we know it.

I found myself rising and looking at Mr.
Moses' body on at least three occasions. Maybe
he had the answer. But he was in a deep sleep
unconcerned with my thoughts. In fact, he
looked so peaceful and noble in Death that
maybe the victory was his. Perhaps, I should
forget it. I again took my seat and closed my
eyes reviewing the scene in my mind. I saw
the charcoal gray pauper's box and it offended
me. Mr. Moses deserved better. I knew I had

to delve into his past for answers.

He grew up in "Pittsburgh", a notoriously tough section of Atlanta located near the AU center. Bootleg whiskey, prostitution, and gambling ran rampant. It was so rough that police, even after integration forced the hire of blacks on the force. Even they avoided it, ignored it. These black areas existed all over America: New York City's Harlem, New Orleans' Callio and Fourth Ward, Charleston, South Carolina's "borough" and "back da Green", and Miami's Liberty City were a few. They had their mores, their own set of rules and no authority was willing to challenge it. They were a colony within a city.

In those days in all black neighborhoods, a black male had to earn status or "street cred". This was accomplished one of four ways: fighting (being good with one's hands), jugging (being a ladies' man), hustling (surviving strictly on instincts and guile) and playing sports. A man child had to be good, not ordinary. Ordinary boys stayed on the porch with Mama, the "big dogs" played in the yard, as the saying stated. These exerted all their energy into their burgeoning masculinity. My friend, Mr. Moses, was one of the these. He earned respect by playing basketball. Accordingly, he "got along" with the hustlers, killers, and "good time women" who ran things in Pittsburgh.

"He was the best I done ever seen!" exploded Ramsey, a childhood admirer. "Nobody! Nobody could shoot a jumper from the post like Moses. All net! Set the rim on fire. I'm tellin' ya! And dribble? Only players close to Moses were Meadowlark Lemon or Curly Neal of the Globetrotters."

Ramsey had just started. His baritone voice boomed like a cannon fire or a broad chested, country preacher at a summer camp meeting.

"Left hand lay up. Hell, he taught Walt Frazier how to lay up! Nobody, I say. Nobody – pro, college, NYC playground, Elgin Baylor, 'Magic' Johnson, Earl 'the Pearl', Michael Jordan – yeah", he paused, "Michael Jordan – nobody was good as Moses Holms!" Ramsey stopped for air.

"Only problem is like all of us, he had to work to help the family, you know. Else he woulda gone to college and the NBA. Made his brothers and sister go to college though, and paid their way through; and "pause" not a one claimed his body. None!" (angrily) "Damned shame!"

After a minute or so, with everyone nodding in agreement to Ramsey's passionate words, Green, with a straight face asked, "Was he hunched over then? With that bulge in his crotch?"

The reaction of the guys was not unexpected. Some went mute; others shook their heads in disgust. Did he really say that?!!! What a helluva question!

"Shit, I just wanna know", Green continued despite sensing the "kick ass" reaction of the guys. "No way he could play ball like that as a humpback. Hell, the Hawks blew that. A humpback that could shoot like Michael Jordan? Phillips Arena couldn't hold the crowd!" he finished with a grin.

Now Green was a regular, retired Navy. He was not unintelligent or insensitive. A well-meaning guy with a poor sense of timing described him best. He sincerely wanted an answer and it came like thunderclaps fraught with lightening intensity.

"Boy you must be a damn fool. Hell no he wasn't no humpback wit' a hernia! The man was long, lean, and straight", Ramsey fired angrily. "Somethin' wrong wit' you boy! You must be on crack!" He looked at him long and hard.

Then disgustedly he said, "You need help. Stupidest shit I ever heard." Ramsey walked to the back and sat at a table, his back to Green. "No offense meant, man. But the Hawks coulda used him," Green quipped. Then he stuck a cigarette in the mouth of his unshaved face and shuffled outside to smoke.

"The man worked forty plus years at Colonial Bakery at night loading bread onto racks. That might have caused it," the Death Angel conjectured with his piercing, trebled voice that irritated everyone. "That kind of work over that period of time could give anyone a hernia or bad back," he concluded and looked around for approval. There was none; there was only disdain for the man had almost succeeded in having Mr. Moses committed as mentally unfit so that he could handle his affairs and take his money.

Some small talk continued for a short time. Another hour or so and the place lay empty except for fat ladies buying expensive ice cream and donuts for even fatter kids – the collusion of Baskin Robbins, Dunkin Donut and Willie Lynch and the genetically naïve single mother buying stock in the company only as a consumer, not a shareholder. Let the circle please be broken.

Green re-entered and took his seat in front of the wall television. The shop lay in good hands, as the regular of regulars kept a constant vigil and would only leave at or near closing, around 9:30 or 10:00pm. What Ramsey had said really piqued my interest in knowing more about Mr. Moses. Mike and Hiram would fill the gaps of whatever lay ahead.

3.

Much to my chagrin, friends and sympathizers began to arrive with their mundane, biblical quotes and annoying crying and sniffling. The real sense of where I was returned in the person of the good natured and ever smiling Leroy. Like always, he was neatly dressed – matching brown trousers and shined shoes, complemented by a burnt orange cardigan and a white shirt. He was probably the only guy at the shop that would look strange had he worn Levis or Wranglers in public. I thought he was a lawyer until he told me different. He was a financial consultant. Briefly, we exchanged pleasantries and then he walked over to the charcoal box.

"Billy and those did a fine job, especially for the length of time he spent in the morgue. Peaceful looking. Moses was a gentleman of the highest order", Leroy ended. We shook hands warmly and he eased out the door to the hallway. Then the trickling really started.

Before I could sit, in came Beverly, uncrowned queen of the donut shop, Buzz, my homeboy by way of Dillon, South Carolina, and Mike (whom I would see later), a robust guy who loved everybody and was anyone's friend, but a stone cold hustler he was and had known Mr. Moses from the 90's. Despite his ever present sneaky / genuine smile, Mike hurt. Moses was his dear friend, an older brother.

Any observer, even a dullard, could feel his pain as he looked in the box. Not a word he uttered. He simply grabbed Mr. Moses' arm gently and touchingly, stared at him for what seemed a long time and, wiping tears from his eyes, strode through the open door to be alone.

By this time Charles had entered the death room. He greeted everyone with words pleasant and somber; "Hi guys! We live in rough times under the sun, but God never makes mistakes." That said, he took a seat near the door. Beverly, who would normally be talking incessantly while chewing gum, acknowledged Charles' words with a whispered, 'Amen.'

She, along with Buzz had moved closer to where Mr. Moses lay. Beverly then peered at the dead man's profile and talked to him. "You in a better place now, Mr. Moses. No more pain and suffering. Now you can rest. All of us gotta follow you someday." She then began to weep and pray quietly as she moved past Charles to the hallway.

Buzz was also loquacious, but unlike Beverly, who would rant on and on about everything and nothing, he preferred verbal battle dealing with the Biblical and philosophical. Whenever he could find a "worthy" opponent, usually Charles, they would fence, then joust, then when it almost seemed they would really engage in a fist-fight, they would stop, always with nothing gained or lost, proven or disproven. Just the thrill of debating for debating's sake.

Now Buzz totally respected Mr. Moses, not only because he commanded respect, but he proved to be the antithesis of what Buzz most enjoyed. Mr. Moses never engaged in debate, be it sports, politics or women. But when it came to the Bible, he considered it sacrilegious. Moses was too well-read about the Bible and treated it as God's sacred word.

"How can ya'll debate the Truth?" he challenged them once. "How can ya'll argue the facts as written by God himself through divinely inspired writers? Don't make sense, ain't that right, coach?" That deep baritone of his sounded like Thunder and I agreed. Needless to say, no one peeped a single word and debate class was cancelled that day and many others.

Accordingly, Buzz peeped into the box with reverence, his premature gray beard and head belying the look of an Old Testament prophet or holy man. He said nothing. He merely nodded his head as a sign to indicate Mr. Moses was all right. He shook my hand, patted Charles on his shoulder and left with Beverly.

Charles and I sat mutely, each

preoccupied with his own thoughts, neither really interested in engaging in conversation. Another visitor entered the room to pay his respects. He was a squat, muscular fellow with a swarthy complexion.

There was a mystique about his mere presence that was hard to explain. He stayed briefly, gave the sign of the cross over Mr. Moses and left. He acknowledged no one and no one acknowledged him. I was told later that the gentleman was a co-worker of Mr. Moses.

After a minute or so, Billy returned and began to give instructions on lining up by car in the parking lot for the funeral caravan.

"What caravan?" I thought. Only Charles and I sat in the death room. "Maybe others were outside", I concluded. While Billy spoke out about cars lining up "the far end of the parking lot", barely muffled sobs and touching lamentations emanated from the hallway, ending his "talk".

Grady entered the room. Attached to his burly arm, barely able to walk came the mournful presence of the Randi. He gently guided her to the charcoal covered pine box where she stood fixated on the face of her dead "Mr. Mos".

She cried real tears, somber tears and her body trembled under the pent up weight of emotions, no longer subdued by hope or prayer or miracle. In front of her, at a 45 degree angle downward lay proof that her friend was indeed dead. The enormity and reality of this truth shook her to the core and she buckled in sheer anguish.

After five minutes or so of this touching display of helpless, hopeless distress, I felt compelled to give her whatever comfort I could. I rose and walked to where she stood. I gently took her by the elbows and led her away from the box. She looked at me forlornly, her face a collage of tears, mucus, duress, and loss. I held her to my chest as best I could and gradually she began to calm herself. Billy handed her some Kleenex and she wiped her reddened nose and eyes.

"Thank you," she managed. "Thank you," she repeated to the both of us. Then she whispered something in Billy's ears.

"Go right ahead," he responded. "Take as many as you want."

Immediately, she reached in her purse and produced a cell phone. She then pushed a button and scrolled to the camera setting. Honing in like a professional, she took several pictures of the dead man, each from a different angle. Everyone present seemed unperturbed by this action, but it shocked me. I had never seen it done before and found it distasteful.

Even a corpse cannot rest until he is in the ground.

No matter, the woman kept shooting pictures until she was satisfied. Then she returned to Grady, a short tan complexioned, big man who stood silently near the door. Like many of the guys at the shop, Grady was an anomaly-his face forbade a frown. Instead, it embraced a smile that could be warm as a grandfather's or cold as a sniper's.

Now Billy had to reconfigure his "caravan" directions. It was brief. Shockingly, there were no others outside. The funeral "caravan" consisted of the hearse and four cars – Billy's, Grady's with the Randi, Charles' and mine – and there would be no police escort. A pauper's funeral was a pauper's funeral and police officers had to be paid. There was no pay here. The grave-site lay five miles away, primarily through residential areas. The mortuary personnel gave each driver the customary funeral sign to place on the dashboard of the vehicle and, as is the custom, told us to switch on the clinking lights.

"Drive as close as possible to the car preceding you!" an old timer cautioned. "You all know there is no police escort so please drive cautiously." I thought that was real nice of the fellow, real classy and definitely on point.

The hearse in place, we fell in behind and, I have to admit, I was nervous. I believe I counted every stop light and stop sign as the processional meandered its way from Second Avenue in Decatur to Cook Road in Ellenwood, all without incident. We made a left turn into the gates of newly finished landfill. This would be the permanent site of Mr. Moses' remains.

## 4.

The place seemed cavernous, all Georgia red clay and covering maybe the length and width of five football fields. This seemed so stark, so cold, so devoid of respect for life. The sun shone bright in the cloudless Columbia blue sky. As I stepped from my truck, I could feel the chill of the March solstice which extended into April. I was glad I had worn my overcoat. Others wished they had.

About nine or so workers stood around, burly young men who, on any given day, became truck drivers, backhoe operators, clay quarry framers or, on this day, gravediggers and pall bearers.

Having coached football, I knew a few of them – great ball players as I remember, but for whatever reason, either by choice or circumstance, they did not play ball in college. Instead, they worked hard at the landfill for a minimum wage.

The service for Mr. Moses had little or no ceremony. His remains lay in the cheap charcoal rug covered pine box without handles or decorations over a six foot deep rectangle excavation with red clay on all four sides. There was no oral prayer, no preacher, no funeral director. There were no words spoken concerning the deceased man's past, present or life in the hereafter. The small gathering, huddled like a group of befuddled spectators, remained mute.

One or two wanted to say something, but no opportunity presented itself in this pitifully organized ceremony. These would experience extreme anguish later in the day and for some time to come. In their hearts they knew they should have bucked protocol and spoke on behalf of Mr. Moses. I still regret it to this day.

The box had been placed on the lowering device directly over the grave. Billy gave a signal to one of the workers and the drab box containing my friend's remains, began its descent. The Randi began to sob again, her body trembling. Grady and the rest of us stood stoically and gazed at the box which disappeared within minutes. Each of us probably said a quiet prayer for the man who would now only be known to anyone who visited as 27/185. These were the numbers placed where a headstone would be to identify our dear, deceased friend.

That designation seemed colder than the East wind which cut through the landfill like a huge razor blade.

"There is a time to weep, and a time to laugh; a time to mourn and a time to dance; a time to reap and a time to sow...'. A smallish woman accoutered in gray, white and black recited aloud these words from the book of Ecclesiastes. She moved from one person to the next repeating words of encouragement and hope. And she was good at what she did. No one disrespected this nun – like woman of God, but as well-meaning her intent, her timing, to say the least, was poor. Where was she twenty minutes ago? Before long, I figured she was sent by the state to recite words of comfort which through endless repetition had diminished its original purpose. It was probably recited over and over before at many funerals for paupers and, in doing so, had lost the personal touch. In fact, she did not know Mr. Moses personally or probably any of the others who endured the fate of a nameless headstone.

Grady, Charles, the Randi and myself left her talking. Only Billy and the workers remained. Grady asked me would I take the Randi to the shop. Of course, I agreed.

"Don't know the way back from here," I

told him.

"Okay. Just follow me. When I turn left on River Road, you turn right," he responded in that deep baritone voice.

"Gotcha," I ended.

We left the landfill almost in the same order as we entered. The only difference was Charles and I had switched places. Grady drove slowly. The winding road was full of sharp curves and blind spots, which I really did not notice on the way there. After a couple of miles, the green and white River Road sign appeared. Grady stuck his thick arm and hand out the window and pointed right. I blew my horn to let him know that I had seen his signal.

I made the right turn and only then did I notice the Randi. She had remained quiet, even composed since we left the "graveyard". She stared straight ahead, locked in her thoughts. Respecting her mute reflection, I drove on to Dunkin. The first thing I noticed when we drove onto the premises was the jubilation of the Randi's daughter as soon as she recognized her Mom in my Tahoe.

"She's not that happy to see me," the Randi broke her silence. "She's glad I back so she can leave. Salena has classes at Perimeter." She then looked at me, her hazel eyes, warm and sincere, "Thank you very much. You my good friend." She grabbed my right hand and kissed it then opening the door, she jumped from the truck to go inside and work.

My eyes followed her into the shop and I thought to myself how brave and resilient the Randi seemed. She came from a foreign country and was in the process of raising two children, both teenagers. Her husband had died and she was alone. I admired her for that.

Then I saw him, the swarthy complected man who came to Mr. Moses' funeral, and he sat at the center table normally occupied by Mr. Moses. We made eye contact but the prisms of the sun on the newly installed windows had played a mean trick on me. I jumped from the truck to go and speak. However, there was no one there. I looked through the window and even cracked the door. There was no one in that chair. Too embarrassed to ask, I left. It could be that I was a little tired from the day's event. In my mind though, I know what I saw. I also knew what I must do. My friend was just put in the ground and no one knew. Every man should leave a legacy. Moses Holms was no different.

While driving to my home, I called Mike and asked him to meet me at Burger King at 5:00 next day. "Do you mind if I record you? I'm writing a story on Mr. Moses and needed your take."

"Depend on it," he replied. "That man was my friend. I'll be there."

## 5.

I could tell he was excited by the energy in his voice. This would be good I thought. And I became excited. I drove up the hill, opened the car door and jumped to the pavement. The house door unlocked, I went straight to where my recorder lay, changed the batteries and checked it for the performance. Fine, just fine. Next, I returned to the front and entered the kitchen. Man, I was thirsty. My super-sized glass, which I kept atop the refrigerator, was soon filled with crushed iced and cold water. I drank in large gulps which soothed my throat, parched from the day's activities. Then I refilled the glass and returned to the bedroom. I placed the glass of refreshing water on the right stand and lay on the bed.

After a few minutes, I thought about Mike. He was what one might call "hood rich". The man had all kinds of "connections", but he was averse to a "9 to 5". Thick and muscular, he was stone street and he loved it. No one could tell this Superfly brother – complete with a black head rag or hair net which held graying hot combed locks, and a 'sexy' smile that hid snaggled teeth – that he was not God's gift to women on the Eastside. Minus the bell

bottoms, he was stuck in the 70's in dress –
full length leather coat with hats to kill and
alligator shoes, spit shined. All in all he was a
likeable guy, good with his hands but one of
the nicest fellows one could ever meet. With
Mike, what you saw is what you got. No
pretentions here and boy did he love Mr.
Moses.

Next day at the appointed time, he and I
sat together in a booth at Burger King. Sixties
music served as a background for my friend's
monologue on Mr. Moses. With the recorder
set, Mike began.

"You gotta understan' now. Mr. Moses
was a good man. He took care of his Mama,
lived wit' her on Simpson Street. He was da
oldest of four children – two brothers and a
sister. Use ta' spoil his sister's children. Took
dem two boys everywhere – ball games, park,
Six Flags. He loved 'em."

"Then one day on the job, he worked at
Colonial Bread on the assembly line – rack
after rack of bread – hard for a black man to
get a job there in dem days, he passed out.
Them folks'll work a man to death an' he was
doing graveyard shift. Twelve, fourteen hours
straight ya know what I'm sayin'? No air, heat!
Spent ten days in Grady."

"Now his Mama had given him Power of
Attorney. In fact, Moses would inherit

everything, you heard? So here we go now!
Make sure that thing's recordin. While Moses
lay up in Grady, his brothers and sister got the
Mama to change the will. They ended up with
everything. Moses ended up with nothin'!
Nothin'!

"When he came back, he found out. But
it didn' seem to bother him. He kept on takin'
care of his Mama. What I didn' know 'til he told
me was they – his brothers and sister – had
different fathers. You know what um sayin'?
Moses' father got killed in a car wreck in South
Georgia. He was wit' 'im. The mother
remarried and bore the other three. That
coulda been a reason they showed no love for
Moses."

"What about the new husband?" I
interrupted. "Did he accept Mr. Moses as his
son?"

"Don't know nothin' 'bout 'im except he
was a hard worker. Ya know what um sayin?
He kept it movin' like most black men during
that time. Anyhow, Mr. Moses..."

"Hold on," I again interrupted. "Did he
have that hump in his back and the bulge in
his crotch in 1994?"

"Yeah, both," Mike hurried. "Jus' wasn't
big like it became. Ima get to that. Jus' lemme
do my thing right now," he said smiling.

"What I was about to say is his Mama died. Within a week, the brothers and sister used some kind of legal stuff and sold the house with Mr. Moses in it! Now that's low down. Dey had to be plannin' ahead. See, he had to scuffle and find a place to stay and bury his Mama."

"Never said a unkind word; found a house on Hightower [Rd] an' we moved his Mama furniture there. Me, Moses and three other fellas. She had some nice stuff. Had big plastic covers over some o' dat stuff. Back then, that meant the item was high class. And Mr. Moses took good care of it."

"How'd you meet him?" I inquired.

"Helped him wit' some yard work one day," Mike replied. "I lived right down the street on the West Side. Would help him with little chores. Tell ya this. He paid better than a '9 to 5' and he fed ya!" Mike paused and smiled that sneaky warm smile of his.

I pressed him now. "Here's what I've gotta know. The hoo-doo, the hump, the bulge. Are they connected?"

"Gotcha'!" Mike jumped on in. "Now Mr. Moses believed that his brothers and sister had put that thang on him. At first, I wasn't buyin' that. You heard? The man lifted racks of bread like I told you. No lettin' up. Rack, after rack,

71

after rack. All that bendin' over and raisin' up with that weight, I believe caused the hump and the bulge. Hernia. That was my take."

"But two things happened to change my mind. First was on Hightower when his do nothin' neighbors stole from him. They knew his work hours. Went through the garage door, climbed the steps and copped a small TV and basketball."

"Moses told me they were in cahoots with his family, so he set a trap. See, ya had to come through the garage and climb fifteen steps to get inside. Man, Mr. Moses put ropes – man, um talkin' dock ropes – that they had to climb over. Used it as camouflage, then he cut the top four steps about three quarters through with a saw. Wanted the cat to hurt when he fell. Pretty good height. Um tellin' ya!"

"Sho nuff, next day there was a dude 'Grady' limpin' and patched up like the mummy. He was mad too. Face all frowned up. Next day, they burnt Mr. Moses out, had him runnin (smile). All his Mama's pretty furniture gone. All Moses saved was the big strapped bag he always carried and the clothes on his back."

Not a week later, Moses had a 'four to twelve'. He leavin' work walkin' to the bus stop. Somebody - he said it was his sister –

roarin' down the street in a small car, lights on dim aimin' straight at 'im. The car was movin' so fast, Moses had to do a Michael Jordan – jump straight up in the air – as the car roared under him. Right then, I began to believe that my boy had the haint on 'im" Mike laughed at this. "Jumpin' like Michael Jordan! I gotta take a smoke. Be right back."

## 6.

That was a great deal of information in such a short time. Shutting down the recorder, I stood, stretched and strode to the front and ordered two big coffees. The lady was nice and cordial.

"I'll have to make a fresh pot," she sang. "Don't get too many orders for coffee this time of the day. Mostly in the morning." It was 5:45.

"Thank you, ma'am. Ain't nothin' like fresh coffee on a cold evening unless it's the company of a fine woman," I teased.

She smiled and I noticed she had perfectly white teeth and beautiful brown skin. A few minutes passed.

"Here you are. Nice and hot and strong," she said. "Cream and sugar?"

"Yes," I answered. "Four creams, eight sugars."

"One dollar and twenty cents!"

I gave her four bucks and walked away. Wished I had more.

"Thanks, sir. Thanks." she happily and warmly said.

Mike had returned and had taken his seat. I presented him with the coffee, sugar and cream and he was grateful.

"Right on time," he said as he sniffed the aroma of the coffee while mixing the cream and sugar. He took a sip and smiled. "Dunkin ain't got nothin' on Burger King. You got the recorder ready? Let's go."

"Now Moses moved to Decatur into an apartment that Charles got for him – 'with his fee attached' – we know how he is. Mr. Moses hated the place an' when the six month lease was up, he moved to a boarding house on Glenwood, then to the house he bought on Flat Shoals Terrace, the one he died in."

"Know what I believe? Cause I went and done somethin' bout it. (Real seriously) and this da truth. As I said, my friend had that thang on 'im, no doubt. A lot o' guys talkin 'bout how he died. Gangrene, 'cause o' leg pus from the plastic, heart give out, tired livin'."

"See, ain't but two of us knew da man – me and Hiram. Ever notice near the end how he struggled, especially when he tried to stand up? Took forever and then he had to stay in one position to get his circulation. The hump had gotten bigger and the bulge, hernia or whatever was the size of a big eggplant. He knew he didn't have long, knew the end was near, but like I said, the man was smart. Retired from his job when he was makin' time and a half. And they had to pay him! Kept plenty money. And he read plenty of books."

"I don't understand. What do you mean? He saved himself from…"

"Don't tell nobody, but Moses had run out of food and I was droppin' off some meat here, vegetables there, sandwiches and stuff. He couldn't make it, walkin' to that store 'en stuff.

This is between me and you now; you know what I'm sayin'? I went to see Queen Mother Mo who live on the West Side. Now follow what I'm sayin' now. She know bout that Hoodoo, or whatever had Moses actin' the way he was. So I gets to explainin' what's goin' on with partna and she whips out dis prayer book."

"Dis will help 'em," she says. "All he got

to do is read it whenever he feel the devil grabbin' at 'im so hear what I'm sayin' now." I said, "Thank ya."

She hit me wit' dis, "That'll be twenty-five dollars."

Mike replied, "Now you know I ain' got no 9 to 5, but I do have twenty-seven dollars on me."

Before I could pull it out, she in my ear talkin' 'bout, "You can work it off, big hunk o' man."

Now ain't that somethin? I don't deal with no senior citizens. Got to be young and firm for Mike!!! You know what I'm sayin'? He smiled that sneaky smile.

"Anyway, I gives her the twenty five and suffer the rest of the week. But in the last package I left at Moses, I put the prayer on the top. Yessuh he fought and he won."

A scowl replaced the slick smile and his calm, carefree manner became viral, vitriolic.

"They shouldn't 'a' gone in that house while he layin' dead and helpless. Nah. Green an' that Randi was wrong. That man, my friend, layin' naked and they go in there an' look! Mr. Moses was a good man, respectful, private. Dey gon' pay!"

He stopped talking, clinched his fists, put his head down and fought back tears.

"It's gon' be all right." I managed to utter. "It's gon' be all right."

Here, I shut down and left Mike to his feelings. No one could deal with them but Mike. He had unmasked his emotional self which was a good thing, but for a tough guy, this side of himself should never be publicly demonstrated as it may be misconstrued as something other than tough. I patted his shoulder and gave him whatever privacy he could garner in a public eating place. Of course, that ended the meeting.

## 7.

The Coffee Shop had reopened by the time Hiram was available. He had changed jobs and his Mom had become ill. Like most guys in the South, he attended to her as he should. We agreed to meet in the back parking lot to avoid interruptions from the guys and eliminate the noise of the coffee shop business. He jumped from his red pickup and opened the door to the

Tahoe where I had the recorder ready. I hoped this interview would answer all the questions about Mr. Moses Holms and hopefully elucidate any confusions surrounding his life and death.

"Gon' get us some coffee. Chilly out here." "Tell Tedeen to put a turbo shot in mine." "Medium?"

"Medium."

And he disappeared into the shadows.

Hiram was street sense cool and tended to his business. Reserved by nature, the robust, light – complected Hiram was closer to Mr. Moses than any of us. Moses had befriended him at a critical time in his life and had essentially "walked him through" with sound advice and thoughtful counseling which saved him from consuming anger and the depression that might follow. In fact, when Hiram arrived as a newcomer to the shop, Mr. Moses was the first to reach out to him. Perhaps he sensed something in Hiram's face or body language that rekindled an experience from his own doleful past. Or maybe he just sensed a kindred spirit in the stout, muscular youngster who was down on his luck.

Because of this encounter, which lasted for several months, a strong bond of trust and respect was fostered. Moses knew that he could tell Hiram intimate things that would not be repeated, and, Hiram could confide his innermost thoughts to Mr. Moses with the utmost assurance that it would not be repeated. Let it be known that Mr. Moses was extremely wary of outsiders and intensely private. Only Hiram and a couple more even knew where he lived, and only Mike and Ramsey knew anything else. At this point, Hiram returned, handed me the cups and climbed into the car. After one sip of the hot, black coffee he began.

"I met Mr. Moses about the same time as you, around 2000. He worked at night at Colonial Bread. Sometimes, he would fall asleep before the midnight shift and I'd awaken him.  The coffee shop had a rule that all customers had to leave by 10:00 pm, but Eliman would let us stay. He was a nice guy, sensitive guy. Mr. Moses would thank me, pick up his newspaper which he placed in his bag – you know that big leather shoulder bag – and either walk the mile or take MARTA to work. He never asked for a ride, never! Don't care how cold it was or wet it was. And he never missed a day or night of work."

Hiram paused here and took another sip of the coffee and continued.

"Now here's the crazy stuff, Mr. Moses and I were sitting in the shop talking basketball –he loved basketball, especially women's basketball. Said they played a pure game, a team game without all the dunking and show-boating of the N.B.A."

"It's a team sport, Hiram!" he would bellow in that deep voice full of passion. "Women pass the ball around, dribble and set a situation to hit the open player, with the high percentage shot. And they play defense – trap game, man to man, three-two zone and they play fundamentals – good footwork, hands up, switch and they glide and use peripheral vision! Ain't that right?"

Naturally, I agreed. Mr. Moses knew the game; I sure didn't.

"Plus, they unselfish. Don't care who score!" he was on a roll now. "Teamwork. That's what I like! The only way to play a team game!" Then he smiled that warm smile of his accented by a perfect set of egg shell white dentures and returned to eating his daily sandwich of ham, cheese and lettuce.

"Here we go now – I had to tell you his love of basketball," Hiram apologized. "Every time he would gesture, you know, make a basketball move, take a shot – in the chair – I would hear a crackling sound, something like wrapping paper, or plastic rubbing together. Mr. Moses had noticed this, saw it in my face. He was sharp now! Real observant. Didn't miss nothin'. Before I could muster the courage to ask, he looked me dead in the eyes and said calmly."

"That's plastic you hear, Hiram. Got it

wrapped from my shoulders to the bottom of my feet. Keep off demons. I don't expect you to understand, but that's all right," he concluded and returned to eating his sandwich.

"Man, I was in shock and just a little scared, but I was cool. You hear things as a shorty about the Boogeyman, the Hoodoo and the Roots, but this was real. It sat right there in front of me. And, I ain't gon' lie, got to me in a personal way. Here sits this man, this good man, my friend talkin' bout being wrapped in plastic 'cause o' demons! And I saw it, or heard it."

Hiram paused here and put his head down for a few seconds. Then blowing in exasperation, he gathered himself and took a gulp of the black coffee. And, he continued.

"Anyway, I got to checking on him more closely just to make sure he was okay. In fact, he let me take him home at night after a while. I was happy because I knew he would get home safely. Always, he would offer me gas money – none of which I accepted. But he offered anyway. I know of several people at the shop who took advantage of his generosity. When he discovered it, because they would talk among themselves, Mr. Moses just shrugged it off."

"It's all right," he would say. "They must need it more than I do. Ain't that right?" he smiled.

"On one Friday night, he asked me would I come by the next morning and get a letter and mail it at the Post Office. Of course, he didn't have to ask. He could have just said, 'Be here!' that's how much love and respect I had for the man."

"You remember how businesslike he was in paying his bills. I have seen him work like that on several occasions at his spot in the coffee shop.

Every piece of mail, every stamp, every receipt – all were handled with the utmost care in an organized manner. (Voice rising) He was independent now. Didn't bother anybody and handled his business. So this letter must be extremely important for he rarely, if ever, forgot anything. Anyway, next morning came and I knocked on his door."

"Who's there?" Mr. Moses' voice grumbled from within.

"Hiram," I replied. "Come to get the mail."

"Okay. Hold on. I forgot," came the hurried reply.

"My second encounter with the Hoodoo or whatever was about to hit me dead on between the eyes and to be honest with you, there is no way I could have prepared myself. The black plastic, covered door swung open. What I saw floored me! No. It scared the hell out o' me."

There stood Mr. Rufus. On his head was something that looked like an inverted lampshade made of heavy rope that tilted awkwardly to his right. There were no teeth in his mouth, his face was shining with Vaseline and his entire body from the shoulders down was covered in the black plastic! Unaffected by the shock on my entire person, he quietly and stoically intoned, "They could be in here too. I know they in the trees. Acha diene dazi poche qat." With that, he gave me the letter and closed the door.

"Man, my legs did not work for a long minute. And I don't scare easily, but that? Along with the incident at the shop and they in the trees? Man! Man! Man! I can't lie and say I believe in the Hoodoo, but then I knew Mr. Moses believed in it and these demons or whatever was after him!

And them words he spoke, I ain't never heard that before! Now Mike talk a 'lot o' trash, but not this time. He was dead on." Hiram uttered visually shaken.

"You okay, my man," I inquired. "This is some great info!"

"Yeah," Hiram somberly replied. "Man, I just don't know. Some things, a man ain't supposed to know!"

Hiram became quiet and just stared into space. It seemed as though he wished to say something profound, something that would make everything logical and tangible that would neatly put to rest all of the mysterious nuances associated with Mr. Moses' life and death. But no! That state of mind could not be reached by logical explanation. And he knew it.

As a fitting substitute, he embraced the idea of catharsis. He was simply relieved to have someone listen to what he had suppressed for quite some time. Totally at ease now, he broke his reverie, stared at me and smiled.

"Man, I'm glad you listened. You just don't know how heavy that was! Thank you (pause) but there is one more piece of information which may help. I know Mike told you about his family - the siblings – but lemme add this."

"Go right ahead, my friend. The recorder is ready," I reassured him.

"Now I know this. Moses believed his family put the hex on him. He told me as much. Listen to this. A couple times, his brothers came to the coffee shop. One was tall and lean, the other was short and thick. Both were clean, but they looked sneaky smug, like they knew something that no one else in the shop knew. They asked Moses how he was doing and always, his reply was cold and pat: 'I'm all right.' Not another word he uttered and he never looked their way."

"The two guys would hang around for a while drinking coffee and eating a couple donuts. They talked to each other in earshot of Mr. Moses who never said a word. Instead, he looked directly at us in a way that said, at least to me, 'if you speak to them, you in it with them, and you against me!' Well, I guess you know, no one acknowledged these guys. Although they were Mr. Moses' kin, they were his enemies. Therefore, they were our enemies as well and, at the time, we didn't even know why."

"Upon leaving, they would approach the coldness and disdain of Mr. Moses' private world very gingerly and utter a barely audible, 'Goodbye. Nice seeing you.' Moses either stared straight ahead or turned his humped back to them. Indeed, his half-brothers did not exist for him. We were always glad when they left – too much tension, so much hate and God knows, not, one of us wanted to be labeled a traitor by the redoubtable Mr. Moses Holms.

"Thanks, my man. You've been most helpful.

Thanks for your time."

"Anything for Moses. That was my boy."
"One last," I interjected. "Did Green and the
Randi go inside the house while Mr. Moses lay
dead on the floor? Mike said they did."

"Yessir, and the Randi prayed. Green
wanted to see if Mr. Moses still had the bulge
in his crotch. They gon' pay for that one. Still
don't understand how the guy who represented
the Medical Examiner's office believed that the
Randi was Mr. Moses' daughter. Ha!" Hiram
half laughed, half cursed. "And then she
prayed over his body. That's the damnedest lie
I ever experienced."

"Did you see his body?"

"Nah. I had too much respect for the
man.

Let's get a coffee. Know you will make it
right for Moses."

I rewound the recorder and I said, "His
story must be told. Our friend just could not go
out as a friendless pauper. He has a legacy!"

"My man," ended Hiram and we walked
toward the shop.

I ordered a medium. Tedeen knew how
to fix it–hot, strong and good. My head still

wasn't right about the last few days of Moses' life other than what Mike had said. But what did happen? I said a warm goodbye to everyone and drove home.

When I opened the front door of the house, it hit me like a ton of bricks. The letter, the letter that Billy gave me, the letter from Moses.

Rushing to the bedroom, I started throwing things around. Where did I put that letter? The bottom drawer on the left hand side of the chest.

I literally ripped the letter open and began to read. I screamed, "This is it! This is it!" I lay on the bed and for the next hour or few hours, I either read or dreamed the story of Moses in his own words; the man himself had recorded his last days on paper. His voice resonated in my mind as he narrated what transpired in his home leading to his death and vindication.

## 8.

"When I began to read the words of the prayer that Mike gave me, I was totally unprepared for what was to follow. All Mike had said was it'll save ya, but he didn't explain a thing. I could feel the end comin' – no appetite, gettin' weak, no interest in television, not even to watch the NCAA tournaments.

The pus in my right leg had begun to fester and I could feel the development of maggots under the skin. The plastic had kept "them" away, but put Moses in a fix. I had no choice but to start the prayer.

As soon as I said, 'St. Michael, the Archangel, defend us in battle...' all hell broke loose. The limbs of the tree over my old bedroom scraped the roof and caused the bed to jump up and down although it was bolted to the floor. The ropes from my traps turned into one, huge, knot- like yarn. Then the demons, my demon, howled and moaned and screeched through my own mouth, my voice a muffle. But I did not quit. Ain't no quit in Moses! And so I continued.

"Defend us in battle, be our protection..." Right here, they roared louder! The sound – I cannot describe. It shook the house and I could hear the tree branches engulf the roof. I could feel it. Man, I am ashamed to say, but I defecated on myself as one of the demons shot through my bowels. He was tiny as my pinky then grew, in front of my face, to 6' 4" or better, with a head like a bull, muscles like The Rock and gripping a sharp ax in his right hand. He stood over me and mocked me.

"Humped back, big crotched, stinking

little man. Do you dare disturb our quiet with your pitiable calls for help in English? You are three times removed from the truth. You must speak in Latin, ignorant nitwit. Besides you need help. We are too many. Bumbling stooge, you are our home sweet home. By the way, your mother was a whore so you are a whoreson."

With that he laughed and bared his sharp fang like teeth caked in dark blood. His piercing red eyes spewed hate. Then insults of all insults: he pissed all over me – hot, stinking piss that burned my skin, then he spat in my face! I became outraged and rose to strangle him. For my efforts, I received a fiendish smile and a slap that took my taste away. Then he became small again and reentered my rectum.

Beaten and humiliated, all I wanted now was to clean myself. I smelled my own stench. Struggling to the bathroom, I wiped myself with toilet paper and paper towels immersed in alcohol and took the longest, hottest shower I had ever taken. I almost wore out that brown soap. For sure, I cleaned all the stink from me.

Even though the noises had ceased and everything seemed normal, I was truly frightened. Fear gripped me like a vise and I felt helpless and hopeless. In my forlorn state, dressed only in my underwear, I remembered what my mother told me decades before. Pray! No matter what the situation is, pray! But not

the prayer that Mike gave me that caused
them to awaken. No. Just talk to the Master.
And so I kneeled at the couch which was my
bed and began.

"Jesus," I prayed, "Please help me, your
fearful servant. Forgive me of all sin. I am
possessed with spirits of the air whom you cast
down from above, eons ago. In your goodness
and mercy, show me the right way to
overcome my dilemma. You and you alone can
do this. Worms have already begun to eat me
even as I have breath. I can feel them under
my skin gnawing and sucking on my
rottenness. Have mercy on your pitiable
creation. In Christ's name I pray – Amen!"

I continued in the manner until dawn,
but my body, so strong at one time, began to
fail me. My mouth became parched and my
muscles cramped. I became dizzy and could
not see. Suddenly, my soul in anguish left my
body and rose through the ceiling. I felt
nothing but relief, but somehow, I did not feel
I died. I became totally relaxed.

My soul rose towards the sky and I
looked down at my crumpled, misshapen body
– hunched back and huge scrotum – clad only
in my underwear. I saw hundreds of imps,
gnomes and creatures I could not name in the
trees that covered and surrounded my house.
These beings were in constant motion except
for larger ones that hung upside down on the

tree limbs like huge vampire bats. From a knotty, thick limb of the tree in my backyard hung a black man, dangling in the wind as a warning to the other black men to beware of the White Eye and his cruelty. The dead man's eyes bulged, his lips and tongue had turned a dark purple and his head tilted grotesquely to the right, his neck snapped by the grip of the noose and the impact that followed. A mob of White Eye men, women and children stood below him in mocking postures. Some of the men grinned callously through tobacco stained teeth. Others drank thirstily from whiskey jugs. All acted like they were at a carnival enjoying themselves. Shame!

Next I saw Native American men, women and children, their ponies taken and sold at auction, walking to Oklahoma. They were ill-equipped for such an arduous journey. Some wore buckskin; others wore cheap White Eye cloth; the rest naked except for beautifully decorated blankets. Some wore moccasins, but a greater number were barefooted. The White Eye Calvary complete with bullwhips, drove the Indians forward. Most would die from exposure to the cold and snow, exhaustion from lack of rest and food and broken spirits, the bane of a once proud people. This was the Cherokee Trail of Tears. I heard their cries and I felt their pain. Although imported from Africa, I was their brother.

## 9.

As I soared higher and higher, the things of the earth seemed so minute, so insignificant. It was at this point, I came to a stop on a grassy knoll on the highest cloud. Here I was frozen in time and steered gently by an unseen hand. I sat fixated in front of a fig tree which had enormous leaves, so thick that I could not see to the other side. Then from within the tree, invisible to my eyes, a voice spoke to me, deep and strong like my father's, gentle like my father's and I was unafraid. It began:

"Greetings, Moses. Welcome to the heavenly realm. I need to educate you on a few important items that can befuddle your extrication from all doubt that hinders your journey. Do you understand?"

"Yes, yes," I fumbled." May I ask your name as you sound like my father?"

"I am he, but as an emissary from YHWH – I AM. Now listen, for my name is nimportant.

First things first, a curse is a term for the calling down of evil on someone or something. It is easy to speak a curse because life and death are in the power of the tongue. Words can bring reality.

Words can bring demonic infestation as

you well know.

"In Ecclesiastes 10:20, the words of a talebearer are as wounds that go down into the innermost part of the soul. When you speak an evil word, a bird of the air will carry it and he that hath wings will speak the matter. But that power only works on those who are not covered by the blood of the Christ and believe in their own power as a person saved by the Redeemer's death, or the cross. Bless! Don't curse. Blessing is a thousand times more powerful than cursing. Again, Moses, this you well know."

"I know! I know!" I repeated with bowed head.

He continued, "We are saved by faith. We do good works because we are saved. Sure, you did many good works, but this is not good enough.

Listen carefully now! The key my dear son is to not only accept Jesus Christ as Savior, but also accept Him as Lord. He must have total dominion over your temple, your mind, your spirit, and your soul. His will becomes your will. This is the only way! The Holy Spirit cannot co-exist with the demons you will fight. When you accepted the demons, the Holy Spirit left because of your choice."

"My! My! My!" I muttered aloud but my

father's voice continued ministering to me.

"These demons normally leave through the mouth, except for the fallen seraphim who excited your anus. This is why you could pray no more. Next time, you will belch and maybe pass wind, but they will leave. I AM has commissioned a helper to say the prayer. Remember this. When they leave, you must invite Christ in the form of the Holy Spirit into your temple else they will return with seven others, far more powerful and terrifying than those who left, do you hear me?"

"Yes," I fearfully responded. "Yes and thank you heavenly host."

"Your faithfulness in acknowledging I AM while you were in distress is thanks enough. You have been given a second chance. You will speak differently. Words that you have never used will come easy for you. The Father blesses you with a new insight of an expression. Return now and cleanse your temple. I will see you soon and do not forget. A helper will follow you. Salaam, shalom, my dear Moses."

Now I was totally alone. The thick fig tree disappeared as vapor as did the voice of my father and the grassy knoll became blue sky. Needless to say, I was quite taken by this event. I knew it happened but... I now steadied myself, and as bravely as I could, I prepared

Moses Holms to mentally meet his destiny.

Soon, I floated on a cloud which conveyed me to my home. The unseen part of me reentered my temple. It was foul. The stench of the demons and the pus and the worms was more powerful than I had fathomed. Heretofore, I, all of me, had accepted this as who I was. It defined my miserable existence as a kind of leper, a boon for unkind jokes from a public that smiled hypocritically with me, then cryptically excoriated and privately demeaned my coming and going.

Now, at long last, Moses Holms would discover himself so his time between the eternities would count for something far greater than a pitiful afterthought. And he would not be without help this time. He would have a deliverer.

Presently, night fell and it was cold. I put a blanket around my shoulders and lay on the couch. I fell into a nervous, light sleep.

## 10.

"Shall we begin, Moses?" a brusque voice interrupted the quiet. "I was sent by I AM to help you."

My eyes strained to see who spoke. Across the room, barely perceptible, stood a squat, powerfully built man with a swarthy complexion. His demeanor reminded me of a Marine drill sergeant – hard, strong, no nonsense.

"May I have your name?" I weakly and awkwardly inquired, trying to sound intelligent.

"That is unimportant, but I am called 'Who is like God'. Have no fear of whatever may transpire. I am ancient and well-schooled in this. We saved the original Moses against the same enemy. And we will save you, his namesake."

"Who is we?" I thought. By this time, I had seated myself facing this man as he again began to speak.

"Repeat after me, Moses Holms. 'From this moment forth, I accept Jesus, the Christ as my Saviour and I accept Him as the Lord of my life!"

This I repeated with all fervor because I truly meant it. And he continued.

"I know and believe that Christ was crucified and died on Calvary to rise again on the third day to atone for our sins and conquer death!"

This I repeated as the demons began to howl and shriek and cuss and make praying difficult. My deliverer continued.

"Forgive me for all arrogance and hate toward my brothers and sister and cover me with the sacred blood of the Lamb!"

When I repeated this, my scrotum swole to a size that tore my underwear then the demon spoke to my deliverer in my voice through my mouth.

He screamed, "Go away, Mikhail!" His voice sounded like a thunder peal from hell. "Go away, Scourge of Satan. Why should you lower yourself to help a lowly indigent as this Moses Holms?

Does not YHWH have more noteworthy labors for you?" He mocked the deliverer and raged on. "Or are you slipping in the hierarchy? Ha! Ha! Ha!

'Who is like God' condemned to serve common man, to run errands as cherubim! We thought you were an archangel?" Then all laughed and mocked in a frenzy. It sounded as a chorus of chaos emanating from my own mouth.

Undaunted by the outburst, the powerful man said simply, "The Lord rebuke you!" And amazingly all became quiet. This amazed me.

This man is powerful I thought. Then he continued the prayer.

"I renounce Satan and all his adversaries. You, I AM, and you alone have all power! You alone are sovereign!"

These words I repeated sincerely and without interruption from the devils.

"Amen!" ended Mikail. "Amen!" I followed. "Now for the purification of the temple, he energetically said, "This is the best part." He smiled confidently." I love doing battle with Satan!"

It shocked me when this hard- looking, warrior-like man smiled. Smiling did not come naturally for him. It shook me, but gave me a confidence I never before had. That changed with his next command.

"Go and clean yourself! You haven't done so since before your first encounter when they misused you. Go! Change your clothes for a new beginning. Pay no attention to the evil ones!"

"Please stand where I can see you," I meekly implored, still frightened to be alone, and rightfully so.

Here, his disposition suddenly changed and he tore into me full of rage. "No!" he roared. "Did you not just place your soul in the hands of the Almighty? Where is your faith, Moses Holms? Or did you, like many others, recite empty words?

Did you confess with worldly emotion rather than confess with the heaven of the heart and soul?

We shall see, won't we? Make the Lord, the Most High, glorified in your victory over the evil one!" At this point, he turned his back to me and I became distraught. Doubt and fear entered my mind as uninvited guests.

## 11.

Shredded by his words, I commenced to do as I was told. Still paralyzed with fear, I took off my clothes and shuffled to the shower. Deep in my heart, I felt that I was still unfit to meet my father in the peaceful place. There was more cleansing I had to endure. My deliverer was right. I had followed his prayer as a frightened victim, not as a sincere believer in true salvation. Alone in the darkness, the demons within began to rejoice, for they knew I had failed to actually believe. Again, they growled and shrieked and tore at my body. The pain in my crotch made my bladder weak and I urinated on myself. Then they pushed the hump of my back to my chest and I threw up.

The vomit was dark blood that smelled of rotting flesh, my flesh. My feet burned to the point that I jumped up and down like I was skipping rope. Then they laughed that hideous laugh of theirs that pierced my very soul.

Suddenly, a powerful force snatched my leg, knocking me to the floor. My dentures popped from my mouth and stopped near the tub. When I reached for them, the grip on my leg tightened like a vise and I was completely under its power. Then all went inky black. Darkness covered all and the force descended into a vast valley of pitch, and I with it.

As I remember, it was vacuous and devoid of life. Then a foul odor saluted my nostrils. I can only describe it as putrid, pestiferous – it smelled of burning, rotting flesh. It was sulphuric in nature and I felt myself swooning then coughing uncontrollably. This foulness continued throughout as I had no chance of escape. I literally flew helplessly downward with no thought of escape.

For relief, I began to focus on the shrieks and screams and helpless cries of despair that filled the vacuum. There must be life, I surmised. How else could these cries of utter helplessness and despair originate? Still, I had not seen anything or anyone and continued my descent. So frightened was I that I did not feel the pain exacted on my own body by the demons until it became overwhelmingly excruciating.

My body hurt and the pain where the demons resided was the most intense. It seemed as though they were redoubling all their effort to exact the greatest agony and torture in their assigned areas. The hump had returned to my back and the demons worked on my sciatica. The pain numbed me from my lower back to my feet. As for my scrotum, it can best be described as a breath-taking continued barrage of kicks by a mule. This made sweat pour from me in torrents. I was in total anguish. My body felt heavy and I fought to stay conscious.

Suddenly we began to ascend. The force that controlled me moved upward in the abyss, I, attached to him like a helpless appendage. I closed my eyes and prayed and it was at this juncture that I became totally aware as to why belief in demons had insulted my Maker and I was still being cleansed. My sin had been gravely disrespectful one. I had literally denied God as God, and in my ignorance, created a world of anger and revenge. Even with this knowledge, I still had to earn my way back into God's grace. That is the stark truth of my wicked unrighteousness. After a short span, a calm settled over me and wonder of wonders, I was soon bodily thrown like a sack onto my bathroom floor.

As I lay, somewhat dazed and stupefied,

a tall figure, dressed in a crimson cape appeared. It was Lucifer himself in his original state. The "Light of the Morning" looked regal, stately, handsome. I was astounded. He looked down at me as a kind of amusing bauble or trinket – a plaything, then he sarcastically asked, "How was the trip to my beautiful domain? Would you like to visit again for a full tour, perhaps even take up residence – permanently?" He glared menacingly into my very soul with that statement.

"My cohorts were afraid. That is why they exerted so much extreme pain in you – to impress me you see! They obviously dislike Abaddon. They would much rather reside in you than take their rightful place in the abyss." He then smiled cynically.

"By the by, I had some libelous, hateful carpenters install a new mirror in your front room. Let's just say, it is a personal gift to my enemy Mikhail. He left this place so many times while you were absent – saving souls you know. And he is good, extraordinarily good. But it gave us time to do our work. I'm sure you will be surprised as well. After all, Moses Holms, you are the protagonist in this Faustian parody." He then smiled grimly and then raising his left arm over his face disappeared in a gray mist.

My heart beat rapidly and my head spun. All this seemed unbelievable. What next? What next? I questioned myself: Was I dead or alive? Did I lose my mind? A dream? No. A nightmare.

While I grappled with my feelings, I saw my dentures lying where they were before the "trip", I grasped them, and while lying on my back, placed them snugly in my bald mouth. Next, I grabbed the edge of the tub and righted myself. It was then I realized that I still had life and set about to do what I originally came to the bathroom to do – cleanse myself. Afterwards, I put on some underwear, a clean smelling tee shirt and my light blue terry cloth robe. Calmed by the warm water and feeling fresh from my toilet, I entered the front room where I was greeted by my deliverer and two assistants from the heavenly realm – Azrael 'Whom God Helps' and angel of transition and Zedkiel 'Angel of Forgiveness' as I discovered.

## 12.

"Good evening, Moses Holms!" my deliverer greeted me. "I have not seen you in a while – twenty four hours to be exact. But I had much to do and so did you. Your experience with them will stead you as we complete our interesting journey. Let me say it has been and will be a unique pleasure for me."

He smiled warmly and always focused and businesslike, he began again. "During the actual exorcism..."sensing a shadow of surprise on my face – "You do know that we three will perform the ritual on you, Moses?"

"Ye...yes," I managed to mutter.

"Now then, during the course of the exorcism, the demons will mortify and, if all goes well, they will leave your body in myriad ways. Therefore, you may cough, sneeze, shake, scream, swear, pass gas, jerk, or burp. Also, there are many things that can happen as they start to exit.

Remember, wherever they entered is where they will leave. Some will be painful, especially those in your scrotum and back. Others will simply whimper as they escape." Mikhail paused, then continued.

"Now you must be cognizant of horrible apparitions and the double talk of the enemy. Do not fear, Moses. This is the devil's way of securing your soul. He will lie and connive so sweet, that you may believe that we – Azrael, Zedkiel, and myself – are the enemy. The same way he has tricked you and others these many years come to bear now."

"I understand," I groaned. "But..."

He put his hand to his lips telling me to

be quiet.

"I am experienced in these matters and the fact that your name is Moses; you have given a reasonable account for yourself; and have more or less pleased the Lord with your good deeds to others. That is why the Sovereign of Sovereigns sent me!"

"So you are Michael?" I dared to ask. "The same!" came the reply. "Lucifer is powerful. He is a staunch, energetic and shrewd being. Please remember he is totally evil. His methods are calculated and deadly. You have seen how he coerced you into anger, pride and blasphemy. Accordingly, I have summoned some friends to help me. Azrael, 'Whom God Helps' and archangel of Transition and Zedekiel, 'Righteousness of God and archangel of Mercy and forgiveness. Also present are psychic warriors which you cannot see."

I thought to myself that this is for real. What had I gotten myself into?

"You see, Moses, we are engaged in spiritual warfare wherein we deal with creatures of the air by putting on the full armor of the Lord. We cannot react like the rash Peter by using a physical force. No. We must pray and follow the example of Christ who when tempted by Satan after 'forty day great fast' He responded to the enemy's temptations by simply saying, "It is written."

"In other words, the Almighty is Sovereign, Ruler of Rulers, Lord of Lords. All bow down in his Presence. This is recorded in all the holy, ancient books. Thus, It is Written!"

"But you said something about armor. Help me to understand this," I implored of him.

"Again, this is spiritual," he said kindly, overlooking my inexperience and ignorance in the matter." We are dealing with those that would like nothing better than to torment you on earth and in the abyss. When Christ was crucified, buried and rose to conquer death and pay for our sins, he left us with the Holy Spirit who gives us a symbolic armor of survival against Satan. And so we have a belt of Truth, a breastplate of Righteousness, the gospel of Peace, the shield of Faith, the helmet of Salvation and the Sword of the Spirit. And we are covered by the precious blood of the Lamb. Does that help?"

"Yes, immensely!" I blurted.

"Let's go!" he intently began. "With me I have Holy Water, sage for smoke, and the candles you see are made of beeswax. They are bright and smokeless. There are seven candles in front which represent the seven orders of angels. The three near the back of the table symbolize the Trinity – Father, Son and Holy Spirit. All of these are offensive to our unwanted friends. The prayer will be recited in Latin because the language is pure, untouched by translation. Satan and his legions detest Latin. The prayer of exorcism will be first, followed by the St. Michael prayer. A one two punch as you say, Moses." Here he smiled at me reassuringly.

Now listen carefully because they are listening too. They cannot discern thoughts, but they can hear us. That's why they're so quiet now. They are attentive because they know their power is limited." And then he spoke louder and bolder! "Because only the Lord is sovereign and you, yes you, must bow down to the Christ of the Trinity for It is Written!"

"We will not go idly by, Mikhail! There are many of us, as many as entered the pigs!" the leader spoke this hellishly through my mouth and I trembled.

My deliverer paid no attention. Instead, he gave his final instructions.

"As I said, they will try to fool you. They do not want to leave you. If they do, which they will, they can either find another victim or go to the abyss. As soon as they leave, we will invite the Holy Spirit to take his rightful place in your temple. That done, they cannot return."

## 13.

Next the three – Azrael, Zedkiel and Mikhail – blessed themselves with the Sign. Then Mikhail came to where I sat, and dipping his fingers in Blessed Oil, began to make the sign on all my sense organs. He began with my right ear, then the left, my eyes – right then left, my mouth, my forehead and nose. He ended at my heart which he blessed with a firm sign. After this, he stepped back a couple of feet and from the inside of his robe produced a small, golden vial of Holy Water. My deliverer then sprinkled the water thoroughly over my head, shoulders, back, chest and crotch.

Almost immediately, the vile beings within me went into a crazed frenzy of shrieking, howling and moaning. Soon, they began to move inside me. They besieged my inner man like a pack of skittering rats, a horde of flying cockroaches, an army of marching fire ants coursing through my veins. I screamed from the pain which only increased with the piercing anguish of fear in my voice.

Here, they defiantly redoubled their efforts in exerting the most excruciating torture imaginable. The severity was dull, gnawing, relentless. I cringed and gasped, and ultimately, I wished for death. In a panic, I cursed Mikhail for dousing me with the water. Lamentably, it availed me nothing. He was so intent on his work that he did not hear me. His focus on the task at hand would not be denied as he had just begun the Invocation for my deliverance. Strangely, the demons became quiet. And I became relieved, at least for the moment. The Latin sounded strange to my ears.

Gloria Patri, et Filio, et Spirituris Sancto Sicut erat in principios Et nunc, et simper et in saecula Saeculorum. Amen

Deus et Pater domini nostril Jesu Christi invocamus nomen Sanctum tuum, et clementiam Tuam supplices exposcimus; Ut per intercessionem Immaculatae simper virginis Dei Genitricis Mariae beati Michaelis Archangelii, beati Joseph ejusdem beatae Virginis Sponsi beatorum Apostolorum Petri et Pauli Et omnium Sanctorum Adversus Santanum ominesque alios Immundos spiritus, qu'ad No cendum humano generi Animasque perdendas Pervagantur in mundo Nobis auxilium praestare Dignares per eumdem Christum Dorminum nostrum. Amen

Here Mikhail paused and he, along with Azrael and Zedkiel, sprinkled the Holy Water around the room. While they cheerily and dutifully worked, the demons began another assault.

During the Invocation, I learned another dreadful lesson as their victim, a warning I should have earlier heeded when I tried to recite the St. Michael Prayer. Any reference to God (Deus), Mary, the mother of Christ, or Michael the Archangel, my deliverer, the demons became extremely violent, more violent than ever, more clever than ever. There must be another word to explain the anguished torment I experienced. I dare say, not blasphemously, that only the Christ Himself could comprehend.

They hit like a sledgehammer, constant and powerful, and, the conniving tribe of Cain attacked structure – all simultaneously – liver shots, heart shots, solar plexus shots – and, oh God, vicious – testicular shots. I squealed like a pig and pissed like a racehorse. I tried to rise and run, but the angels, believing that I might hurt myself, had fettered me to the chair. Breathless, from the blows, I doubled over, my throbbing head touching my legs. What tortured me more than anything was I had allowed them to enter me and take abode. I became both a host and a victim. Contempt for myself raged.

Frrrrrt! Phhst! Rrrriiipp! I began to pass gas like a howitzer blowing from my behind. It seemed to last forever! Phhst! Fffwappa! Here, I knew the demons were exiting my rectum because it hurt, it burned. The sensation can best be described as a constipated bowel movement. After the initial blasts, it felt like I was defecating bricks, but I knew it was only

110

gas, foul smelling like rotten eggs or stagnant water. Sweat poured from me and my heart raced within. How much longer? How much longer?

## 14.

"Relax, Moses Holms," Mikhail said calmly. "Relax. We are nearing the end."

And then he spoke firmly and nonsensically to the demon within me." Who are you? What do you want? Your friends are leaving. Soon you will be alone. One on one with the Almighty, one on one with One who makes hell tremble. Oh, I can feel your fear, your anguish!" then my deliverer boomed, "Who are you and what do you want in the blessed and precious name of Jesus Christ!"

There became a total silence. Azrael and Zedkiel prayed intently. This seemed to be the focal point of this drama after a short time, Mikhail began again, "What is your name and state your business with Moses Holms."

"In the name of the risen Savior we pray!" enjoined Azrael and Zedkiel.

Soon, a voice, deep and cavernous, emanated through my mouth and, again, I felt helpless. There was nothing I could do to hinder it. All my efforts were concentrated on the idea of breathing through my nostrils. The demon spoke, "I want to make this creature of YHWH suffer beyond the stoning of Stephen and the torture at Golgatha. I want him to curse his Creator then I will give him life in death. I want him to play with Black Shuck and roll at pins with Judas, Stalin and Hitler. Ha! Ha! Ha!"

He then turned his full attention to my deliverer. Slowly, grimly, and hatefully, he continued.

"Then I want you, Mikhail! Yes, you. Look away disdainfully if you will. Your time is at hand. You who threw Lucifer from on high and since lived a charmed life lauded by all. Yes you!" more virulently now.

"You will be subdued by one who is less in rank, but more powerful in hateful resolve, less in strength, but more versed in Machiavellian cunning, less in celebrity but far more notable in devious treachery. 'Who is like God' – Ha!"

Unmoved by the prideful boasts and attacks of the demon, Mikhail weighed in, "Again, I ask, what is your name?"

"I am...Ah no! Not now. We're having too much fun. At least I am," the demon mocked. Then he changed tactics as he now spoke to me.

15.

"Look at the mirror yonder, Hump,"he mocked. "Your father wants to speak to you. You'll be interested to know that he has a thing for you that Mikhail, with all his power, dare not give," he chided. Here the demon grabbed my chin and, with a powerful grip, positioned my head where my eyes could only gaze at the mirror.

A figure, not unlike my father, appeared and began to speak. The voice sounded like the tender, caring, manly bass of my Dad. He began.

"When you left, I did some research. I discovered something that I did not know. You loved a woman, a Hindu woman who did not love you back because of her culture. I sought the help of a friend and he fixed it. Look for yourself!"

There she was! All I ever wanted. Her hazel eyes so soft and amorous; her skin – tanned and flawless; her smile – coy and alluring. She had loosened her barrette and her lustrous, black hair flowed in the breeze. Her shapely body for which I had longed for so many months, years shone perfectly through her sheer, white gown.

She saw me and beckoned me forward.
Blushing, she smiled in that coquettish, teasing
way of hers and sang out, "Come on Moses. I
turn back on culture." (The broken English
made it sound sweeter). "I want you. I take
care of you and Meester Holms. Come! Let's go
away!"

All my manhood rose within me. I felt
like I would explode from thoughts of endless
pleasure. I gasped with desire and tried to rise
from the chair but the restraints contained me.
Then the figure of my father spoke again.

"Come on over, son. See? I told you.
Here she is. All that stuff I told you about a
second chance were honest blunders of mine.
Your old man made a mistake. I'm sorry. I
thought I was protecting you. I know you don't
wanna hurt no more. Listen. Here's the truth.
They hurtin' you harder because of Mikhail. He
ain't your friend. Come on with the woman.
You see she loves you," he chuckled.

"Listen, Moses. My friend offers life in
death, not life after death!" here I was
confused and the figure of my father sensed it
immediately.

"All you have to say in Latin is
Abrenuntio Deus. That's all. The Randi and life,
son! Come on!  Abrenuntio Deus!" he blurted.

"What does that mean?" I asked, more confused than ever. But I never heard. The demon shut my ears to sound. All I could do was read the lips of the figure of my father.

"De furnace ferrea! In the name of the Lord God of Hosts: de fornace ferrea!" With these words, Mikhail vehemently commandeered the baleful situation. He knew what I had sensed and restored order. The beast within uttered not a word; I regained my ability to hear; the drama of the last few moments would reach its conclusion, thanks to Mikhail.

Thereupon, I exerted all my energy to clearly discern what the semblance of my father had said. At this point, I didn't know what to believe - was this my Dad or not? But I did not want to have any doubts or regrets here. "Deus," I knew. The other word – even with pretty good lip reading – confounded me. And so again I turned to Mikhail, who had already sensed my dilemma,

"Abrenuntio," he pronounced. "Ah-bree-noon- see-oh!" he slowly repeated. It means 'renounce' in Latin. "By the way," he paused, and, in his glib manner of speaking continued. "By the way, you do agree that a mirror reflects what it sees, do you not?"

"Yes," I agreed.

Then he pointed behind me and chortled, "Look. I believe you two know each other."

I turned my head and behold, right before my unbelievable eyes stood Lucifer – tall, imposing,, even regal – accoutered in a lustrous black robe with red silk inlay and pure white ruffles which served to grimly accent the searing, distended nostrils of his cruel aquiline nose and cavernous amber colored eyes which pierced and absorbed the entire scene. The "thing" snarled and hissed and his dusky, serpentine figure appeared all the more menacing. But wonder of wonders, as soon as our eyes met, he raised his left arm covering his personage, and disappeared in a cloud of gray smoke. This shocked me to my senses – that is, what senses remained.

I remembered what Lucifer had said about "changes" in the mirror. I recalled the terror of the awful and dizzying descent into the infernal darkness and desolation of the abyss. I recollected how rudely he treated me upon my return. He threw me as a discarded, worthless play thing on to the bathroom floor, then stood over me and mocked me as I pitifully and blindly groped for my dentures in the inky blackness.

Did not Mikhail warn me that he was cunning and evil and relentless in his attack on the Lord's creation, mankind? I then looked from Azrael to Zedkiel to my deliverer, Mikhail.

What a powerful man, a good man, and an angel of faith. For the first time in this ordeal, I felt special, chosen.

This sense of security emboldened me and I looked at the mirror and yelled with all my might: "Abrenuntio Satana! Abrenuntio Satana! I renounce Satan!" Next, I broke into a spasm of uncontrollable sobbing. My tears, so long checked by fear, anger, torment, anguish – poured freely and steadily much like the deluge of a summer rainstorm.

Through my tears I saw the Randi, the love of my life, turn into a decaying corpse, her dead eyes and bloodless mouth became portals where greedy maggots disgustedly rolled, squirmed and crawled as they gorged themselves with the rotting flesh. Her black hair, once so full of lustre that it shined in the sunlight, became gray and weblike and gossamer. Then she, already dead, swayed as if alive, and fell silently to the floor.

As for my "father", he became a swarm of dead flies that stunk like sulphur. Then he, like Lucifer, turned into a gray mist and disappeared into nothingness.

## 16.

"So you dare to embrace the enemy, eh Moses?" came the menacing voice of the demon. "You silly shell of a man! You toad! You joke. Ignorant wretch, do you not know that even as I speak, there are those who are still using you.

Your tax return? Remember? You signed it away! In that petty, little shop, with its petty little people, your name is associated with foul smells and tawdry jokes. Your "friends" never liked you; they liked your money! No one even claimed your wretched body. Your family denied your existence! The Christian creatures of I AM – such hypocrites. Pauper! Not even a funeral. Your grave has no name on it. And yet you profess your love for Him." And then brazenly, "Call YHWH and see if he comes!"

"It is written!" Mikhail boldly and loudly interrupted. "It is written!" he commandingly repeated. And the demon became silent, totally silent. Relief swept over me. In this entire ordeal. I had never been berated so viciously. Ironically, the harshness of the demon's damning words became my epiphany. Everything became clear – all at once.

"Stupid me! All this time passed! All this pain endured and it took this one moment to realize that I had grievously sinned. I hated by siblings for slighting me. I blamed them for placing this curse on me. I abhorred the way they had controlled my very existence. And forgiveness, yes forgiveness, was not part of the equation. This was what Mikhail had alluded to as my revelation and vindication.

"Sure, I took care to give to those in need; I counseled those who sought my help; and I spoke well of God in the midst of the egghead Dunkin biblical scribes. With the help of my deliverer I even accepted Christ as my Lord and Saviour. But truth be told, I had a heart of stone, unforgiving and relentless in the pursuit for revenge and, during this quest, I became my own victim through pride and lust.

I had sinned against my Creator, but, through it all, He never gave up on me. He even sent angels to steer me to ultimate salvation. Here I was at both the lowest and highest point of my life. To say I was broken and undeserving would be an understatement. To say I had to totally lean on I AM became the reality. Accordingly, I asked my Redeemer to eradicate my heart of stone and unforgiveness and replace it with love and liberating forgiveness. Here I called aloud my siblings' names and knew that my Lord had accepted my confession. I gave thanks. Now I fully understood the pain of pain and the enormity of my sin of eliminating the presence of the Holy Spirit and inviting the takeover by the demons. Here I received the Peace that surpasses understanding.

"Now to the end," a gleeful Mikhail began and the three of them signed themselves as he began a prayer.

"Father in heaven, give us the faith, courage and stamina to expel this demon and any of his cohorts that remain from the temple of your servant and creation, Moses Holms. As we put on the full armor of YHWH, guide us as we do your will for your glory by diverting this soul from sheol to the Beautiful Place, from satan to your bosom. Amen!" (in unison).

All paused here and girded themselves in various spiritual armor: Mikhail dawned a purple scapular around his shoulders and, in either hand, carried the Holy Book and a golden vial of blessed water; Azrael, hooded like the Grim Reaper, held the cross of Raphael and a maroon Holy Book; Zedkiel held a silver vial which contained the balm of mercy and forgiveness in one hand and, in the other, a small red bible emblazoned with gold letters. Then Mikhail again began to pray, this time directed at me.

"Because he has contritely confessed aloud and before witnesses the sin of the unforgiving heart and humbly implored forgiveness from the Most High YHWH, we consecrate your creature Moses Holms by placing upon his spirit the full armor of the

Lord, Jesus Christ. Thusly, we give him your Belt of Truth, your Breastplate of Righteousness, your Gospel of Peace, your Shield of Faith, your Helmet of Salvation and your Sword of the Spirit. Amen" (all).

Here Mikhail sprinkled me with blessed water and what I expected, happened. The beast within me, as long quiet, came to life and kicked me in my stomach. Immediately, I began to throw up an inky, tar – like substance, but I felt no pain.

As I choked and vomited, Mikhail only smiled. I flushed with embarrassment. Zedkiel rushed to the bathroom and returned with a towel. He commenced to clean me as well as he could.

Even I knew now that the last of the demons were escaping. And I became relieved. Mikhail now began the prayer of exorcism. I will deliver all I can remember with the help of the kind Spirit.

17.

Psalmus LXVII Exsurgat deus et dissipentur Inimici ejus: et fugiant qui Oderunt euma facie ejus.

Sicut deficit fumus deficiant; Sicut fluit

cera a facie ignis, Sic pereant peccatores a facie Dei

Gloria Patri, et Spiritui Santo, Sicut erat in principio, et nunc Et semper, et in saecula Saeculorum. Amen

Now! Mikhail passionately urged this time in English:

"We cast you out, every unclean spirit, every satanic power, every onslaught of the infernal adversary, every legion, every diabolical group and sect, in the name and by the power of our Lord, Jesus (Holy water splashed on me) Christ. We command you, begone and fly far from the Church of God, from the souls made by God in His image and redeemed by the Precious Blood of the Divine (holy water on Moses) Lamb. No longer dare, cunning serpent. To deceive the human race, to persecute God's Church, to strike God's elect and to sift them as wheat (Moses sprinkled). For the Most High God commands you (Moses sprinkled) He to whom you once proudly presumed equal; He who wills all men to be saved and come to the knowledge of Truth command you (1 Timothy 2:4).

During the exorcism Moses' body contorted and swing back and forth. He spoke in strange tongues – Hindi, Hebrew, Aramaic and Greek. Mikhail, Azrael and Zedkiel focused on the task and did not permit or were impervious to distractions.

"God the Father (sprinkling on Moses) commands you! The Son of God (sprinkling) commands you. God, the Holy Ghost (sprinkling) commands you! Christ, the Eternal Word of God made flesh commands (sprinkling) you, Who humbled himself, becoming obedient unto death (Phil 2:8) to save our race from the perdition brought by your envy. Who founded His Church upon a firm Rock, declaring that the gates of hell should never prevail against it and that He would remain with the world (Matt 28:20). The sacred mystery of the Cross commands you, along with the power of all mysteries of Christian faith (sprinkled). The exalted Virgin Mary, Mother of Jesus (sprinkling) commands you, who in her lowliness crushed your proud head, from the moment of her Immaculate Conception...

"Thus cursed dragon,... we adjure you by the living God, (sprinkling) by the true God, (sprinkling) by the Holy God, (sprinkling) by the God who so loved the world that he gave up his only Son, that every soul believing in Him might not perish but have life everlasting; (John 3:16). Cease deceiving human creatures and pouring out, to them the power of eternal damnation!

"Who are you?" Mikhail boldly stated emphatically. "Name yourself!"

"Never, Mikhail! came the reply.

Then 'Who is like God' switched to Latin and the first and ancient words poured from him like scorching heat.

"Vades satana, inventor et magister omnis, fullaciae, hortis humanae salvtis. Da locum Christo, in quo nihil innvenisti de operibus luis; da locum Ecclesia Uni quam Christus ipse acquisivit sanguine suio. (sprinkling)

Then with perfect timing, Mikhail effectively switched to English.

"Stoop beneath the all powerful hand of YHWH, tremble and flee when we invoke the holy and terrible name of Jesus, this name which causes hell to tremble –

"Who are you? Speak demon! This name to which the Virtues, Powers and Dominations of heaven are humbly submissive; this Name which the Cherubim and Seraphim praise unceasingly repeating: Holy! Holy! Holy is the Lord, the God of hosts" (sprinkling).

In an ironic twist, Mikhail called to Azrael and Zedkiel to bring their bibles to where Moses, beleaguered and exhausted, sat. The three of them feverishly loosed the tightly tethered leather bands that had binded Moses Holms in the chair. Upon Mikhail's impassioned command, Azrael pressed his Bible on Moses' back, Zedkiel...on Moses' chest and Mikhail placed a golden crucifix on the bulge of the perplexed and bewildered Moses Holms.

Mikhail, with his most powerful and most commanding tone, declared, "Come out of this temple, demon. Give me your name. In the name of Jesus the Christ, the Son of the Most High YHWH, say on!

18.

After a silence that seemed centuries long, the demon icily spoke: "I am Soneillon!"

"The demon of hate," rejoined Mikhail. "Leave this man who is the Creator's own.

Dragon-like and horrific, the demon Soneillon slowly slithered through Moses' mouth. Prideful, even in defeat, he evilly displayed his final act of defiance against I AM and the three angels. In his powerful jaws for "viewing", was the freshly ripped and bleeding scrotum of Moses Holms. In a like manner, impaled on spike like horns that protruded from both sides of his neck, rode a yellow, fatty, distended appendage which was formerly Moses' hump. When Soneillon's tail finally exited, Moses collapsed to the floor.

Immediately, Azrael and Zedkiel came to his aid and began to pray: Come Holy Spirit, fill the hearts of your faithful and kindle in them the fire of your love, especially your servant Moses Holms. Send forth your Spirit and they shall be created and You shall renew the face of the earth.

This secured Moses' temple. The Holy Spirit, so long absent, took His rightful place in Moses' being. Azrael positioned himself at Moses' head and Zedkiel kneeled at his side in an attitude of prayer.

## 19.

Across the dimly lit room, Mikhail faced Soneillon alone. The demon, in a final display of empty boasting and futile bravado, began to transform himself into his original form, the sight of which had intimidated mankind since the time of Adam.

From the figure of the dragon appeared two enormous hooves leading up to enormously powerful legs connected to a muscular torso. Fantastically, four powerful arms, each with clawed hands, complemented the upper portion of his body. One pair of arms occupied the normal position while the other pair protruded horrendously from his back. The head stretched forward from the neck with a thin line of horse – like hair on top. Remarkably, it was purely skull without any skin and lacked a nose. Long, carnivorous teeth, two large horns protruded from both sides of the neck and diabolical, crimson red eyes completed the 8'6" tall figure.

"And so we face each other," the demon began. "Throne vs. Seraphim and Apostate vs. believer. Don't trust yourself, heh, Mikhail? Azrael is a Seraphim. Zedkiel is a Cherubim. Both deal directly with the salvation of souls. I deal with Charon and sheol. You people have so little faith!"

He paused, hissed, then meandered on. "Never thought of you as being so short and dumpy. I AM's Modus operandi is to amuse himself by having the dregs of society fawn on Him, depend on Him, love Him for doing favors. This is why the weak, the desperate, the atypical – like yourself: diminutive, sawed off, stubby, hardly handsome – who would believe that you threw Lucifer from heaven – you. He can control you and you love it. And so the ignorant, the unclear, the outcast, the zealot reign supreme as 'chosen ones': the apostles, your lepers, your Mary Magdalene, your Stephen – stoned to death for what? Belief in Christ? What a fool! All fools! And you! Foolish, blind little man. I could destroy you right now as I killed yon pauper, Moses Holms. But the Second Coming draws nigh and I will seek you out and…"

At this juncture, Mikhail interrupted the hapless demon's monotonous diatribe by cheerfully intoning, "You must, be thirsty? Here. Have some refreshment." With that he threw the contents of the remaining viles of blessed water on the figure of Soneillon knowing that the water acted as a slow burning acid on the demon's skin. Then he continued.

"It seems too dim in here," Mikhail continued and forthwith proceeded to raise the shades of the window and rip out the black garbage bags "Some light based energy from the Evening Star, Venus might help," he smiled.

The pure light caused Soneillon to pitifully bellow like a caged lion then scream like a castrated bo hog. He pitifully began to clumsily half run, half crawl to escape the searing pain of the light. With terrible grunts and groans – Ohhh! Ooooo! Ahhhh! That resounded seemingly throughout the entire world with their volume.

Suddenly, inexplicably with no warning, came these powerful and deadly words that rose above the din: Vade retro satana! Vade retro satana! Vade retro satana! To the astonishment of all rose the bass voice of Moses Holms. The words he bravely uttered with its pure genuineness and power, condemned Soneillon to the abyss.

128

Blotched and bloody, the demon became a puff of charcoal colored smoke that disappeared through the open window.

Mikhail, smiling, looked to where Moses lay. Azrael had cuddled his soul as carefully as a newborn when it left his mouth. Zedkiel had prayed the final words of absolution. Mikhail now walked over and said simply and solemnly: "And with his final words, Moses Holms secured his reservation in the Beautiful Place. Both Azrael, with Moses' soul held securely, and Zedkiel took passage into the crystalline light of Venus. Only Mikhail and Moses' temple remained. The powerful angel filled with admiration, soberly and tenderly cleaned the lifeless body and then he too took leave. Only Moses Holms' lifeless form remained.

## 20.

"Hey, playa! Thought you done gone back to New York. How da story comin? Wanna see wha' I tol' ya in print! Ha, ha, ha!" This was slick Mike being Mike. Big Joe strolled in – all 6'6" and 240 pounds of hard life muscles and chain gang savvy. "Hey, Stump!" he blurted. Thought I had to bring the "five blind boys" (clenching his humongous and rough fist) round your way and straighten things. "Everything good?" he smiled that warm, semi-toothless and always guarded smile of his. "You okay?" I nodded yes.

"Shut up, boy!" came the ever jive time, always joking voice of Darryl. "You ain't gon' do nothin'!" Then he pulled a pocket knife from his coat and told Joe, who had sat near the window," come on, Big Boy. Um' buying all wolf tickets tonight and you the biggest wolf:" Darryl smiled.

"See, dere you go," interjected Joe, "And don' be smilin'. You jus' like a cabbage – all head an' no ass! A real man don' need no knife! Go sit down somewhere 'fore I pull off yo' leg and whip you wit' it!" Everybody in the shop exploded with laughter. After a few minutes, Darryl pulled Stump aside and whispered.

"Some strange lookin dude been askin' for ya. Said he got sup' m' for ya. Looked like some kind o' foreigner. Knew you though."

"Thanks," Stump replied. "I'll handle it." He didn't seem concerned. No. He just found a comfortable spot and sat on an uncomfortable chair and shot the breeze with his boys. He sipped on a steamy turbo-shot medium that Jack had sent from behind the counter. Others drank iced tea; others drank green tea; still others drank plain water. All had a story except him and James.

Both were quiet by nature and naturally introspective. Life had made them loners. Through the years, they had experienced some tough times but survived. Older and wiser, they preferred their own company. But the myriad and mostly raucous sampling of the fellows at the shop – they came from all walks of life – provided a refreshing perspective, comfort, amusement and renewal of the joy of living life at all costs.

After an hour or so of listening to mostly jaw jacking and stunting of the guys, Stump signaled to Jack that he was leaving. Jack then made the usual small cup with Splenda and gave it to Stump. He thanked him, said his goodbyes to the fellows and left. The cup was hot, but Joyce would be expecting it

## 21.

Outside, he walked to his car, a '95 Toyota Camry and thought about his Tahoe that had been totaled in a wreck.

"Never did like that truck much," he thought aloud. "No integrity in workmanship. Just never felt comfortable in it."

Inserting the key into the door of the Camry, he could only think of finishing his story. He felt so close to the end. He leaned in to place the hot coffee in the beverage carrier. Then he heard a voice, not threatening, but different. Momentarily, he thought for his safety because he was in a vulnerable situation. And he knew from experience that this should not be, he was too street smart for this.

"Turn around. I am sorry I startled you," came the voice, warm and congenial. With this, Stump relaxed and did as he was requested. Right there he met Mikhail face to face. As he began to speak, his manner was akin to meeting a dear old friend with whom one had shared a lifetime of warm and meaningful experiences. It reminded him of telephone conversations with his brother, Frank.

"I am Mikhail, 'Who is like God'. You as a scholar, know of me, but you don't know me. According to your calendar and your history books, I am ancient. Even your sacred books – the Holy Bible, the Holy Qu'ran, the Talmud depict me as being here from the beginning of the world as you know it.

"There are many truths, half-truths and blind ignorance concerning my origin, my stature, my physical appearance, etc. I will not address all; however, I will clarify a few of these erroneous perceptions. As you see my face is not like lightning; my eyes are not torches; my skin is not burnished bronze and I do not have a belt of gold nor does my voice sound like a multitude. I am not tall and graceful to behold. Instead, I am short; I am stocky; but, above all, I am a warrior, tried and proven on the greatest fields of battle.

As such, my demeanor is normally stern, my speech brusque, I only smile when actually fighting Lucifer and the apostate angels or helping those whom Satan may hurt such as your friend. I was thrilled when commissioned by YHWH to settle the dispute about the location of the secret burial site of the original Moses. You see, Satan wanted the secret revealed to the Israelites for reasons that were diabolical, evil. The Prince of Lies tried to ensnare me by using words of chicanery, words that became personal. As always, I deferred to my Creator, I Am and rebuked satan in His holy Name.

"Now your Moses," and here he paused, "Your Moses was a special case. He died seeking. This idea is special to YHWH and so He, in his faithfulness to mankind commissioned me, with help to your Moses who now lives with other believers in the Wonderful Place. He suffered much physical pain because of angelic help and his own worldly indiscretions, but his soul is with the saved," he assured Stump.

"Relax, my friend. You haven't said a word since I began, but please rest assured, your efforts in saving the man Moses speak volumes of your character, your charity, and your unselfishness. Are you not headed home to finish your story? 'Well,' (in a timely reference to an important line in the piece) 'IT IS FINISHED!' Then he smiled. By the way, I enjoyed playing a part in your work and please tell your friends Mike and Hiram, they made me laugh. Peace and blessings. I now take my leave as the harvest is great and the laborers are few! Ha, ha, ha!"

Mikhail then opened the door to his vehicle, cranked the motor and drove away. What Stump had just experienced was a manifestation miracle. I Corinthians 12:11, Paul.  He had literally been chosen as a witness to bring God glory. This frightened him because he considered himself unworthy, not ready. But there it was in the personage of Mikhail, one of I AM's own. Not one to trifle long with what is real, he accepted what just transpired as fact. It was too late to call Colin, his son. To tell him what he had witnessed so he did what Mikhail had literally said. The story is finished, now go home and rest. The harvest is great, but the laborers are few. He had work to do. Plus, Joyce's coffee had gotten cold.

# ABOUT THE AUTHOR

William "Buck" Godfrey was born in April of 1943 in Charleston, S.C., Godfrey is the oldest of four sons. He graduated from Burke High School, where he played football and baseball and earned scholarships in both sports to Delaware State. He played center field and hit .511 in 1965 at Delaware State while serving as captain of both teams as a junior and senior and helping the baseball team to three CIAA conference championships.

After trying out for the New York Mets and stepping into the ring to participate in Golden Gloves boxing, he began to use his degree as an English teacher in Manhattan at Spanish Harlem Junior High School 120 in 1967.

After moving to Georgia to earn a master degree in English from Atlanta University, his first coaching job came in 1974 as the B-team football coach and head baseball coach at DeKalb County's old Gordon High School (now McNair Middle School). His baseball team went 26-4 in his second year while leading the Generals to the semi-finals.

He later coached at Towers High School from 1976-1982, coaching B-team football and leading the Titans as offensive coordinator on the varsity. He also coached swimming and led Towers to a second-place finish behind Dunwoody at the DeKalb County Swimming and Diving Championships in 1978.

In 1983, Godfrey became head coach at Southwest DeKalb High School. He was coach at SWD for 30 seasons and won the 1995 Class AAAA Georgia High School Association state championship, runner up in the 1990 finals, won 13 region titles, and has posted a 273-89-1 record. Thus, becoming the winningest football coach in DeKalb County history.

Most importantly, off the field he has helped 267 former football players and trainers get college scholarships. 17 of these were kickers or punters alone – 216 of those are college graduates with 27 earning master degrees and 7 doctorates. Of this, at least 8 have gone to play in the NFL. He also saw many former swimmers continue their education as well.

Godfrey is also a published author and has written three books: Moods of a Black Man, Songs for My Father, and The Team Nobody Would Play. The latter was a book about his own experience as a Little League baseball player in 1950s Charleston, SC.

He is a member of the Omega Psi Phi Fraternity and is an inductee of the Delaware State Athletic Hall of Fame, the Atlanta Sports

Hall of Fame and the Georgia Athletic Coaches Association Hall of Fame.

While pursuing his interests in sports and building self-esteem and character in youth, he enjoys fishing and has been married to Joyce Godfrey for 48 years and resides in Decatur, Georgia.

# MORE BOOKS BY WILLIAM "BUCK" GODFREY

The Team Nobody Would Play

Coming in 2017

My Friend Eddie Robinson
The Worthington Valley Dolphins
My Friend the Hound